COUNTRIES OF THE WORLD

Libya

Gareth Stevens Publishing
A WORLD ALMANAC EDUCATION GROUP COMPANY

About the Author: Paul A. Rozario is a graduate of Oxford and London universities. A professional writer and editor specializing in Africana, he has lived and worked in East Africa and has written and edited books on Kenya, Tunisia, Nigeria, and Liberia.

Written by
PAUL A. ROZARIO

Edited by
MELVIN NEO

Edited in the U.S. by
**MONICA RAUSCH
RICHARD AND
PAT SWETALLA**

Designed by
JAILANI BASARI

Picture research by
**SUSAN JANE MANUEL
THOMAS KHOO**

First published in North America in 2004 by
Gareth Stevens Publishing
A World Almanac Education Group Company
330 West Olive Street, Suite 100
Milwaukee, Wisconsin 53212 USA

Please visit our web site at
www.garethstevens.com
For a free color catalog describing
Gareth Stevens Publishing's list of high-quality
books and multimedia programs, call
1-800-542-2595 (USA) or 1-800-387-3178 (Canada)
Gareth Stevens Publishing's fax: (414) 332-3567.

© **TIMES MEDIA PRIVATE LIMITED 2004**
Originated and designed by
Times Editions
An imprint of Times Media Private Limited
A member of the Times Publishing Group
Times Centre, 1 New Industrial Road
Singapore 536196
http://www.timesone.com.sg/te

Library of Congress Cataloging-in-Publication Data
available upon request from publisher.
Fax (414) 336-0157 for the attention of the
Publishing Records Department.

ISBN 0-8368-3111-X (lib. bdg.)

Printed in Singapore

1 2 3 4 5 6 7 8 9 08 07 06 05 04

Contents

AN OVERVIEW OF LIBYA

Libya is an ancient land with a history dating back thousands of years. A land of deserts once teeming with animals and lush with plant life, Libya sits at the crossroads of Africa, Europe, and the Middle East. Many empires, including the Greek, Roman, and Ottoman empires, have left their influences on the architecture, art, and religion of the country. In spite of its rich heritage and the friendliness of its people, Libya has few visitors. Since the 1970s, the regime of Colonel Mu'ammar al-Qadhafi has had disputes with many foreign governments, and, as a result, Libya and Libyans have been isolated from the rest of the world. At the start of the twenty-first century, however, Libyans and foreigners hope that Libyan culture, art, and hospitality can be enjoyed by all.

Opposite: **The old town of Ghadames is still well preserved. Whitewashed walls, often seen in desert areas, shield people from the fierce heat of the sun.**

Below: **Libyans treasure relationships and spend their free time with friends and family, either at home or over a cup of tea in a tea shop.**

THE FLAG OF LIBYA

The present Libyan flag is solid green in color, and was adopted in 1977. It is the third flag that the country has had since becoming independent in 1951. When Colonel Qadhafi came to power in 1969, he changed Libya's flag to resemble Egypt's flag of liberation. Libya, however, broke off diplomatic ties with Egypt when the Egyptian president went to Israel for peace talks. Libya's flag then was changed to this solid green flag. The color green is considered a symbol of devotion to the Islamic religion.

5

Geography

Libya occupies a total of 679,182 square miles (1,759,081 square kilometers) and is situated on the coast of North Africa. Libya borders the Mediterranean Sea to the north, Egypt to the east, Sudan to the southeast, Chad and Niger to the south, Algeria to the west, and Tunisia to the northwest.

Highs and Lows

Libya has an average land elevation of 600 to 2,000 feet (200 to 600 meters) above sea level. The country forms part of the vast North African plateau that stretches from the Atlantic Ocean in the west to the Red Sea in the east. The highest point in Libya is Bikku Bitti, or Bette Peak, rising 7,438 feet (2,267 m) in the Tibesti Mountains along the southern border with Chad. The lowest point in the country is south of the coastal town of Marsa al Burayqah at a place called Sabkhat Ghuzayyil, with an elevation of 154 feet (47 m) below sea level.

Below: **Most of Libya's terrain consists of flat to undulating deserts, with occasional plateaus and other rocky outcrops.**

6

Geographic Regions

The Libyan terrain is divided into three separate geographic regions: Tripolitania, Cyrenaica, and the Fezzan region. Located in the northwestern part of the country, Tripolitania gently rises from the Mediterranean coast in a series of terraces until it reaches Jabal Nafusah, a mountain plateau that rises between 1,968 to 3,000 feet (600 to 915 m) above sea level. Along the way, the land passes through the Jefara Plain, which covers 5,998 square miles (15,535 square km). With its many oases, Tripolitania is the most important agricultural area in Libya and also the most populated region. The capital city of Libya, Tripoli, lies on the northern coast of Tripolitania.

Cyrenaica is located in the eastern part of the country and is separated from Tripolitania by the Sirte Desert, along the coast of the Gulf of Sirte. The important cities of Benghazi, Al Bayda, and Derna are situated in Cyrenaica. Almost 90 percent of the country, including the southern part of Cyrenaica, is dominated by the Sahara Plateau, a desert region with scattered oases, such as Jalu.

In the Fezzan region in the southwest, sand dunes formed by the constant wind can reach as high as several hundred feet and stretch some hundred miles in length.

Above: **Oases with clean drinking water and lush vegetation are a welcomed resting place for travelers making their way across the harsh and dry deserts of Libya.**

BENGHAZI
The history of Libya's second most important city dates back to the sixth century B.C. Benghazi is in the Cyrenaica region and has an interesting mix of Arabic, Italian, and African influences.
(A Closer Look, page 46)

Climate and Rainfall

Libya's climate is affected by the Mediterranean Sea and the Sahara Desert. The coastal areas in Cyrenaica and Tripolitania experience a Mediterranean climate. Summer temperatures in July and August range from 104 to 115° Fahrenheit (40 to 46° Celsius) in Tripolitania and between 81 to 90° F (27 and 32° C) in Cyrenaica. Winter temperatures along the northern coastline average 52° F (11° C). Temperatures in the south average 100° F (38° C) in the summer and 63° F (17° C) in winter. Day and night temperatures also vary significantly. In summer, the day and night temperatures in Tripoli average 86° F (30° C) and 62° F (17° C) respectively. In winter, the day and night temperatures are about 61° F (16° C) and 47° F (8° C) respectively. The highest temperature recorded in Libya was 136° F (58° C) at Al 'Aziziyah.

Rainfall is low in Libya, and some places do not receive any rain. Rain tends to fall in a short period of time during the winter and can cause flooding in northern Libya. Rainfall averages between 16 to 20 inches (400 to 500 millimeters) in the northeast, to less than 5 inches (127 mm) in most of the south. Desert regions hardly get any rain. Droughts are common and occur every five or six years. Droughts can last up to two years at a time.

Above: Areas located along the coast, such as the ancient city of Sabratha, enjoy a mild climate all year round that supports the growth of vegetation.

TRIPOLI

The capital city of Libya plays an important role in the economy of the country and is the center of communications and trade. Tripoli also has a rich heritage, and the oldest part of the city includes ruins of buildings from Roman times.

(A Closer Look, page 70)

Plants and Animals

Libya has very little vegetation. In the hot, dry south, some hardy plants grow on the desert's edge. At oases, however, the presence of underground water helps support date palms, acacia trees, tamarisk trees, pistachio trees, and henna plants. Tripolitania and Cyrenaica have a Mediterranean climate that supports grassy plains called steppes. Not much of these steppes remain, however, as they have been turned into agricultural fields. Some forests of thorny scrub and short juniper trees cover the mountainous areas of Cyrenaica. When enough rain falls, plants like the asphodel and grasses such as the esparto grow in the northern regions of Cyrenaica and Tripolitania. Farms along the northern coasts of Libya produce barley, oranges, figs, dates, lemons, olives, and apricots using a network of irrigation canals.

Libyan animals are well-suited to life in the arid regions of the country. These animal species include foxes, gazelles, guinea pigs, hyenas, jackals, jerboas, leopards, skunks, and wildcats. The country is rich in insect life, and locusts and butterflies move about the interior of the country in swarms. Bird species in Libya include partridges, wild ringdoves, larks, vultures, hawks, eagles, and prairie hens.

Many animals are used in Libya in agriculture. Libyan farmers keep horses, goats, sheep, donkeys, and cows. The most important domesticated animal is the camel. Riding camels also is the preferred way of moving about the desert for many of Libya's nomadic communities.

Above: **Although the harsh climatic conditions of Libya's deserts support little vegetation, hardy plants manage to take root and survive.**

FOXES AND ANTELOPE

Not many large animals live in the wild in Libya. Some foxes and antelope, however, have adapted to the climate and make their homes in the country.

(*A Closer Look, page 52*)

Left: **Reptiles are a common sight in Libyan deserts. Reptiles found here include lizards (*left*), chameleons, and poisonous snakes.**

9

History

Archaeological evidence for settlements and crop cultivation in present-day Libya dates back to between 8,000 and 6,000 B.C. Once home to moist savannas rich in animal life, the southern region supported small groups of hunters and gatherers. As this region gradually became desert, many people moved toward the coast or to desert oases. Between 2,700 and 2,200 B.C., groups of immigrants called Berbers from southwestern Asia came to the area and settled along the coast, as well as in the country's interior.

Arrival of the Phoenicians and Greeks

Phoenicians from present-day Lebanon arrived by sea in about 600 B.C. and founded three settlements in northwestern Libya: Lepcis (later called Leptis Magna), Sabratha, and Oea (present-day Tripoli). The region's Roman name *Tripolitania*, which means "land of three cities" in Latin, refers to these first settlements. The main Phoenician city was Carthage, in present-day Tunisia. As Carthage grew in power, Tripolitania came under the control of the Carthaginian empire. Greek immigrants from Crete and other islands in the Aegean Sea arrived in Cyrenaica from the seventh century B.C. onward. They founded the cities of Cyrene, Barce (present-day Al Marj), and Euhesperides (present-day Benghazi).

THE GARAMANTIAN CIVILIZATION

The Garamantians were an indigenous people who lived in the Fezzan region of southwestern Libya. Archaeologists today are working in this region to excavate ruins from the ancient Garamantian civilization.
(A Closer Look, page 54)

THE LIBYAN DYNASTIES

Between 1,500 and 1,000 B.C., the Lebu tribe living in the Cyrenaica region made several raids on Egyptian territory to the east. A warlike people, many of the Lebu eventually settled and worked in Egypt. In about 940 B.C., some of these early Libyans came to power in Egypt and proclaimed themselves pharaohs, or rulers, of Egypt and Cyrenaica. The Libyan dynasties of Sheshonk and Osorkons are known as the twenty-second and twenty-third dynasties of Egypt.

Left: Sabratha is one of three ancient settlements founded by the Phoenicians. This settlement site is of archaeological importance and has been preserved and restored over the years, as illustrated by the beautiful ruins of this theater.

Left: In ancient times, settlements were often built on higher ground, so they could be better defended from invaders. The ruins of Yafran's old town sit on a rocky bluff from which the town's citizens were able to see attackers as they approached.

From Roman Rule to Arab Invasion

By 96 B.C., the Romans had taken control of Tripolitania from the Carthaginians and Cyrene from the Greeks. After the Romans converted to Christianity, they brought this new religion to North Africa. The region generally thrived under the Romans, and Septimius Severus, a Libyan from Leptis Magna, even became emperor of Rome in A.D. 193. Roman rule in North Africa declined in the fifth century onward, with the conquest of North Africa by Vandal tribes from Europe. Although Rome was able to reconquer North Africa, the region eventually fell into the hands of invading Arab tribes from Saudi Arabia in the seventh century.

Arab tribes brought Islam to North Africa in the seventh century. Further immigration of Arab tribes into present-day Libya took place in the eleventh century. By this time, most of the Berber population had mixed with the Arab population and converted to Islam. Between the ninth and the sixteenth centuries, the region was ruled by a series of Islamic dynasties based outside the area: the Aghlabids of Tunisia, the Fatimids of Egypt, the Almohads of Morocco, andthe Hafsids of Tunisia. European powers, such as the Normans of Sicily and the Spanish, briefly controlled parts of present-day Libya in the twelfth century and later in the sixteenth century.

ANCIENT CYRENE

Cyrene was the most successful city established by the Greeks along the Mediterranean coast. As an important trading center, the city had great wealth, and the Greeks constructed many lavish buildings. Cyrene was also a center for Greek learning.

(A Closer Look, page 44)

Under the Ottomans and Qaramanlis

In 1551, present-day Libya came under the control of the Ottoman Empire in Turkey. The Ottomans established the region as a province and ruled it from Tripoli. The official in charge of the province, called a *bey* (BAY), was chosen from the influential tribes of Tripoli to rule as a governor and collect taxes on behalf of the Ottoman Empire. The region continued to prosper from the trans-Saharan trade that took place within its borders. Turkish soldiers stationed in the province also married local women.

In 1711, the province's bey, Ahmad Qaramanli, took control of the province from the Ottomans. He took the title of pasha, and his family ruled until 1835. During this time, European powers, such as Great Britain and France, began fighting for control of the Mediterranean Sea. Pirates also patrolled the North African coast and attacked trade and military ships. Piracy along the North African coast ended in the first half of the nineteenth century when the French and British navies fought the pirates. The Ottomans regained control of the region in 1835 but encountered resistance from the Sanusiyah, an Islamic group founded in Cyrenaica in 1837. Ottoman rule came to an end in 1911, when present-day Libya was invaded by Italy during World War I.

THE ITALIAN OCCUPATION

Italy occupied the area of present-day Libya for over thirty years in the early twentieth century. Since the region's peoples strongly resisted Italian rule, the Italians treated them with much brutality, resulting in many deaths.
(A Closer Look, page 60)

Left: This illustration depicts Tuareg nomads meeting in the deserts of what is today Libya. It is taken from a book by Englishman G.F. Lyon, who lived and traveled in Tripolitania in the early part of the nineteenth century. Lyon's book gives an account of the customs and landscape of North Africa in the early nineteenth century. The Tuareg in the picture ride maherry camels, which are camels specially bred for speed. Maherry camels have shaved heads and necks, as well as legs that resemble those of racehorses. They are said to be able to cover 900 miles (1,448 km) in eight days.

Occupation and Independence

During World War I, Italy declared war on Turkey and claimed many Turkish possessions in North Africa, including what is now Libya. After the war, Italy was given control of all of present-day Libya, except for the interior of Cyrenaica. From 1922 onward, the Italians tried hard to crush all local opposition to their rule, opposition that was led mainly by the Sanusiyah. Thousands of Italians were sent to colonize the area, and the locals were pushed off their farmlands and into the inhospitable desert. Entire tribes were also imprisoned in camps. The whole region came under Italian rule by the early 1930s, when the leader of the opposition, Omar al-Mukhtar of the Sanusiyah, was captured and executed.

During World War II, the Allied and Axis powers fought in the region. The scene of the greatest battles was Tobruk, which changed hands several times during the war. Italy lost control of the area after the war. Britain and France administered the region for a few years. On December 24, 1951, Libya was declared an independent monarchy under the rule of King Idris I of the Sanusiyah. Oil was discovered in Libya in 1959 and quickly came to dominate the country's economy. On September 1, 1969, King Idris I was deposed by a military coup, and the country was declared a republic.

Above: **The Tobruk Commonwealth War Cemetery in eastern Cyrenaica, near the Egyptian border, marks the site of several important battles fought during World War II.**

Below: **King Idris I (1890–1983) was the first independent monarch of Libya.**

13

Libya under Colonel al-Qadhafi

The Libyan Arab Republic was run by a committee called the Revolutionary Command Council, headed by Colonel Mu'ammar al-Qadhafi. Colonel Qadhafi has ruled Libya since 1969 and has attempted to increase Libya's influence around the world. In 1973, and again in 1980, Libya occupied part of northern Chad. The territory was eventually returned to Chad in 1994. In 1979, Libya sent military aid to the government of Idi Amin in Uganda. Throughout the 1970s, 1980s, and 1990s, the Libyan government has been accused of supporting violence and terrorism in countries such as Morocco, Egypt, Sudan, Tunisia, Gambia, and Nigeria. The Libyan government also allegedly supported terrorist organizations in Japan, the Philippines, and Germany. In 1992 and 1993, the United Nations imposed sanctions on Libya for failing to hand over two Libyans suspected of bombing an American passenger jet over Lockerbie in Scotland. Libya eventually handed the men over for trial in the Netherlands in 1999. Since then, tensions between Libya and the international community have eased, and, in mid-1999, the U.N. sanctions were suspended. These sanctions were eventually lifted in September 2003. Libya, however, has been branded by the U.S. government as being part of an "axis of evil," a group of countries seeking to obtain and use biological and chemical weapons of mass destruction.

Left: **Posters depicting Colonel Mu'ammar al-Qadhafi, Libya's head of state, are found all over the country. Qadhafi had humble beginnings; his parents were desert nomads. He joined the army and, in 1969, led a coup that brought him to power.**

Septimius Severus (145–211)

Born in Leptis Magna in the Tripolitania region of Libya, Severus became a member of the Roman Senate in 175 and a consul member in 190. He also served as governor of various Roman provinces, including Sicily. Following power struggles and political assassinations in Rome, Severus's troops proclaimed him emperor in 193. His homeland benefitted greatly from Severus's reign as emperor as he embarked on an ambitious building program in Leptis Magna. He expanded the port facilities, built a new basilica and forum, and constructed the Via Colonnata. Some of the buildings built during Severus's reign and their ruins can still be seen today.

Septimius Severus

Omar al-Mukhtar (1862–1931)

Born in Cyrenaica, Omar al-Mukhtar attended an Islamic school established by the Sanusiyah religious brotherhood. He had very strong religious beliefs and felt it was the duty of every Libyan to rebel against foreign control of the country. This idea led him into direct conflict with the Italians, and he fought them when they invaded the region in 1911. Later, in the 1920s, when the Italians used more repressive measures to deal with the Libyan resistance, al-Mukhtar was able to unite many different tribes into an effective army. Al-Mukhtar personally led the resistance for almost ten years, before being captured in 1931. He was tried and convicted by the Italians and executed.

Mu'ammar al-Qadhafi (1942–)

Born to a Bedouin father, Qadhafi was a good student who showed an interest in politics while still at school. After graduating from the University of Libya in 1963, he joined the Libyan military academy. As he rose through the ranks, he plotted to remove Libya's King Idris I from power. Qadhafi seized control of the government in September 1969 and has ruled Libya ever since. From the 1970s onward, Qadhafi's government has allegedly supported and funded terrorist activities. Years of international condemnation of his activities and economic and political sanctions on Libya have reduced the extent of Qadhafi's support for terrorism. Western governments, however, still remain suspicious of his regime.

Mu'ammar al-Qadhafi

Government and the Economy

The official name of Libya is the Socialist People's Libyan Arab Jamahiriya. *Jamahiriya* means "state of the masses," referring to the idea of government ruled by the people. The Revolutionary Command Council, formed after the 1969 coup to govern the country, was replaced in 1977 by the General People's Congress (GPC). The GPC consists of over 1,000 members, who are themselves elected by people's committees lower down in the hierarchy. Local Government is carried out by grassroots committees called Basic People's Congresses, which can be found in every village, town, and city.

Legislative and executive powers lie with the GPC, which meets for two weeks each year. The work of the GPC is carried out by the General Secretariat and the General People's Committee. This committee functions as a cabinet of ministers responsible for various areas such as transportation and education. The head of government, the secretary of the General People's Committee, is elected through a series of people's committees. The last elections were held in March 2000.

Left: **This building houses the Central Bank of Libya. The country's official name in the Arabic language is Al Jumahiriyah al Arabiyah al Libiyah ash Shabiyah al Ishtirakiyah al Uzma.**

A new head of government, Shukri Muhammad Ghanim, was appointed in June 2003. In practice, however, Libya continues to be run by Colonel Mu'ammar al-Qadhafi, who is considered the chief of state, although he has no official title. Qadhafi is also the head of the armed forces. Many people believe the government of Libya, in practice, resembles a military dictatorship.

Libya is divided into 25 *baladiyat* (bah-lah-DEE-yaht), or municipalities. The Basic People's Congresses administer local government and rule with the help of officials.

Legal System

Libya's legal system is based mainly on Islamic law, called *shari'ah* (sha-REE-yah). Summary courts try minor crimes and cases involving small sums of money. Courts of first instance judge cases that involve larger sums of money, as well as appeals from summary courts. Appeal courts are for serious crimes and appeals from courts of first instance. The Supreme Court is the final court of appeal. Supreme Court judges are appointed by the GPC. The Supreme Court can also try cases of a legislative or constitutional nature. Other courts in Libya include military courts and people's courts.

ARMED FORCES

Libya requires military service of all its citizens, although the rule is often not applied to women. Many military officers hold government positions and their influence in political matters is strong. The armed forces in 2000 consisted of 35,000 personnel in the army; 9,000 in the navy; and 22,000 in the air force.

An Oil Economy

Libya's economy is dominated by oil, which was first discovered in the country in the late 1950s. By 1977, Libya was one of the world's largest producers and exporters of crude oil. In 1999, oil provided more than 99 percent of Libya's export earnings and contributed one-third of the country's gross domestic product. The revenue from oil production and exports has made Libya one of the richest countries in Africa, but the oil industry only employs about 2 percent of Libya's workforce. In 2001, Libya earned an estimated U.S. $13.1 billion from exports, most of it from oil. Libya's peak oil production of 3.3 million barrels per day occurred in 1970. Since then, production has fallen due to a drop in world demand. Oil output in mid-2003 stood at 1.5 million barrels a day.

Agriculture, Mining, and Manufacturing

Before the discovery of oil, Libya had an economy based on agriculture, with 80 percent of the population employed as farmers and animal herders. By 1999, however, the agricultural sector employed only 18 percent of the workforce and contributed less than 10 percent to Libya's gross domestic product. Major

OIL: LIBYA'S GOLD
The discovery of oil in Libya has had a great impact on its economy and has made the country one of the richest on the African continent.
(A Closer Look, page 64)

FOGGARA: TRADITIONAL WATER MANAGEMENT
Communities living in the deserts of North Africa have developed unique ways of harnessing groundwater for farming and other needs.
(A Closer Look, page 50)

Left: **The Esso Standard Company was one of the first foreign oil companies to set up operations in Libya. The company began operations in the late 1950s.**

Left: As the capital city of Libya, Tripoli's international airport and seaport (*left*) are among the country's most important. Tripoli is also well linked by a road network to other parts of the country.

agricultural products include wheat, barley, olives, dates, citrus, vegetables, peanuts, soybeans, beef, and mutton. Libya, however, imports about 75 percent of its food because the country's agricultural production is unable to meet its needs.

Libya's mining industry focuses on oil extraction. Minerals such as gypsum, sulphur, salt, and potash are also mined. The manufacturing industry in Libya centers on oil refining, but also includes textiles, cement, and food processing. Other non-oil manufacturing industries include steel, iron, aluminum, and petrochemicals production. These economic activities contribute about 20 percent to Libya's gross domestic product.

Transportation

Libya has a network of paved and unpaved roads that link all parts of the country. The country has 15,215 miles (24,484 km) of highways, including a 1,132-mile (1,822-km) coastal highway that follows the Mediterranean between Libya's borders with Tunisia in the west and Egypt in the east. A north-south highway links Sabha to the coast, and other highways connect Murzuq, Ghat, Nalut, and Ghadames. Libya's national railway system was shut down in the 1960s, but the country has plans to revive it.

Libya's main seaports are Tripoli, Benghazi, and Tobruk. Marsa al Burayqah has a seaport terminal from which crude oil can be exported on large containerships. The country's main international airports are at Tripoli and Benghazi.

THE GREAT MANMADE RIVER PROJECT

Because water is a scarce commodity in the desert, the Libyan government has embarked on an ambitious engineering project of deep canals to bring underground water to areas that face a water shortage.
(*A Closer Look, page* 58)

GHADAMES
Designated a World Heritage Site by UNESCO, Ghadames boasts rich examples of desert architecture that shows how the region's ancient people developed resources to adapt to the environment.
(*A Closer Look, page* 56)

People and Lifestyle

Libya has a population estimated at 5,499,074 in July 2003. Ninety-seven percent of the population belong to the Arab-Berber ethnic group, while much of the remainder consists of communities of Greeks, Maltese, Italians, Egyptians, Pakistanis, Turks, Indians, and Tunisians. The population also includes about 166,510 non-citizens, the majority of whom are Africans working in Libya.

A Young, Urban Population

Libya has the fastest population growth rate in North Africa and one of the highest on the African continent. Between 1995 and 2000, the population growth rate was about 3.3 percent. It has since slowed slightly, with the 2003 population growth rate estimated at 2.39 percent. Nevertheless, this relatively high growth rate has resulted in a young population, with about 35 percent of Libyans below 14 years of age. Sixty-one percent of the population is between 15 and 64 years of age.

Left: Libya's population is highly concentrated in the country's urban areas. In 2000, an estimated 88 percent of Libyans lived in urban areas. The majority of urban Libyans live in the capital, Tripoli, and Benghazi, the second largest city in Libya. In 2000, about 1.5 million Libyans were living in Tripoli, while Benghazi had a population of 1.1 million Libyans.

Families and Clans

Family and clan associations are strong in Libya. Every Libyan knows to which clan, or tribe, he or she belongs. Clans are called *qabilhah* (kay-BIL-lah) and are often descended from a single ancestor, sometimes originating hundreds of years ago. The clan is headed by a *sheikh* (SHAKE) who is considered the authority in his respective clan. Sometimes clans form alliances with other clans in the same region or form alliances through marriage. This grouping of distinct but related clans is called a *leff* (LEEF).

The basic groups within the clan are individual families. Called *bayt* (BAIT), these families include aunts, uncles, cousins, brothers, and sisters, as well as grandparents and great-grandparents. In rural Libya, the extended bayt live together in the same house or a collection of houses built close together.

Migration

Since Libya's independence, people of other nationalities have come to live and work in the country. In 1992, there were nearly two million foreigners living in Libya. Many of these foreigners were oil workers, refugees, or illegal immigrants. Today, foreigners, especially Africans, continue to come to Libya in search of work.

A DIVERSE MIX OF PEOPLE

Libya historically has been home to many immigrants: Greeks, Romans, Phoenicians, and Africans. The Arab culture associated with Libya today arrived between the seventh and eleventh centuries. Turkish soldiers also arrived in large numbers when the country was part of the Ottoman Empire. At the height of the Italian occupation in the twentieth century, as many as 70,000 Italians lived in Libya, although the number has fallen drastically since then. Libya also had a small Jewish community that was established many centuries ago, but most Jews have since left the country.

Traditional Lifestyles

Although the majority of Libyans lead a relatively modern way of life in cities and towns, a small number of rural Libyans still practice traditional lifestyles. These Libyans include the Berber, Bedouin, and Tuareg communities.

Pure Berber communities can still be found in pockets of the Jabal Nafusah region, south of Tripoli. The Berber can also be found around Suknah, Zouara, and Ghadames. The Berber speak their own language as well as Arabic. Berber communities still follow tribal laws and practices.

The Tuareg are found near Ghadames and Ghat. Unlike Arab Libyans, the Tuareg place more emphasis on inheritance from the maternal side of the family, rather than the paternal side. Tuareg society is hierarchical and has distinct classes and groups.

The Bedouin are Arab nomads and herders that wander Libya's deserts. Previously numerous all over Libya, Bedouin communities are getting smaller as more of their members move to cities to find work. The few Bedouin who continue with their traditional lifestyle move with their herds of camels and goats from oasis to oasis and set up camps in large tents.

THE BERBER

The Berber are a group of indigenous people found in North Africa. Although they are Muslims, some Berber customs and beliefs have their roots in pre-Islamic times.
(*A Closer Look*, page 48)

THE TUAREG

The Tuareg are a semi-nomadic people with their own language. Although some Tuareg still live in the desert (*below*), many of the Tuareg now live in villages and towns.
(*A Closer Look*, page 72)

Left: Libyan women have made much progress in the areas of education and employment. Although the family unit is still important to women, today many women work in professional jobs that contribute to the country's economy.

Other groups that lead traditional lifestyles in Libya's remote desert regions include the Sharifs of Fezzan, a religious tribe that claims to have divine powers, and the Marabouts, who are known for their mystical dances and chanting.

Women in Libya

Women have always been an important part of Libyan society. Even in traditional societies, such as the Berber and Tuareg, women can own and pass on property to their offspring. The role of women in Libya today is slowly changing from being wives, mothers, and homemakers to being businesswomen and professionals. In 1969, women obtained full legal rights and the right to vote. The government encouraged women to pursue an education and enter the workforce after having children. Working mothers were offered cash incentives, and day care centers were established, making it more attractive for women to return to the workforce. Laws were also enacted to ensure equal pay between men and women working at the same jobs. More and more women are becoming professionals as a result of these changes. Women also serve in the Libyan army and are active in charities and social organizations.

ANCIENT AND MODERN WAYS

Although many Libyans live in urban areas, they have not lost the customs and practices of their ancestors, many of whom lived in rural areas. Many city dwellers still wear traditional clothes and eat traditional food. Many urban Libyans also marry in the traditional way, based on the rules of the arranged marriage, where parents find partners for their children. Urban Libyans have the advantages of modern life, but they still hang on to older customs and values.

Elementary and Secondary Education

Libyan children attend nine years of compulsory elementary education. School starts at the age of six, although some children attend preschool classes between the ages of four and five. Elementary education is divided into three stages: the first stage lasts four years; the second, two years, and the third, three years.

Secondary education is optional for Libyan children. Those who wish to continue studying do so for a further three or four years in order to obtain general, specialized, vocational, or technical certificates. With these certificates, Libyan students can then enter a university. Military training is part of the curriculum from the secondary level onward.

Learning at Home

The Libyan education system offers homeschooling to children who live too far away from schools. Students on this program receive their education via special radio and television broadcasts. A tutor or parent provides the basic tutoring. Students then take the same examinations as their counterparts who attend regular school.

Below: All students who attend elementary school in Libya study the Arabic language, the Qur'an, science, the arts, and mathematics.

Left: Libyan schoolgirls walk home after their school day in Sabha.

Higher Learning

Undergraduate degrees at Libyan universities take three to six years to complete, depending on the subject. Degrees in medicine and engineering take a longer time to complete compared to degrees in Arabic literature and geography. After completing a basic degree, students can do postgraduate studies to obtain master and doctoral degrees.

Libya's first university was established in 1955 in Benghazi. Called the University of Libya, it had an enrolment of 31 students studying in the areas of arts and education. Over the years, the university added several other areas of study, including engineering, medicine, law, agriculture, and science. In 1972, the university was partitioned; those faculties based in Tripoli were grouped under a new university called Al-Fatah University, while those in Benghazi formed the new University of Garyounis. The Al-Fatah and Garyounis universities continue to be Libya's leading universities today. Other universities in Libya include the Omar al-Mukhtar University, Nasser University, Tahaddi University, the University of Derna, and the Bright Satr University of Technology. Institutes of higher learning also include the National Scientific Research and Study Center.

QUR'ANIC EDUCATION

Libya's education system also includes Qur'anic schools. These schools offer boys the chance to study the Qur'an, the Islamic scriptures, outside of regular school sessions. Students must complete three years of elementary school before enrolling in a Qur'anic school. The next six years are then spent following a syllabus that combines religious education with a normal academic program. Qur'anic education involves memorizing the Qur'an and other Islamic texts, such as the Hadith, which are the sayings of the prophet Muhammad, and academic discussions about the Qur'an.

Islam

A large majority of Libyans — about 97 percent — practice the Islamic religion. Although Islam is the official religion of Libya, freedom for most other religions is guaranteed. The remaining 3 percent of Libyans are predominantly Christians of various denominations, including Protestants, Roman Catholics, and Greek Orthodox.

Islam was founded by the prophet Muhammad, who lived in Saudi Arabia in the seventh century. Followers of the Islamic religion are called Muslims. Muslims believe that God, or Allah, speaks to his believers through prophets, including people such as Abraham, Moses, and Jesus. Muslims believe that Muhammad is the last of this line of prophets. They believe in one God, angels, and a judgment day, when Allah will decide who goes to heaven and who goes to hell. The religion teaches its followers to do good deeds in order to reach heaven. The holy scripture of Islam is the Qur'an, which Muslims believe was dictated directly by Allah to Muhammad. The Qur'an is written in classical Arabic and has not changed since it was first written down in the seventh century.

THE JEWS OF LIBYA

Until recently, Libya had a significant Jewish minority dating back to the third century B.C. During the Italian occupation, 21,000 Jews were living in Libya. When World War II broke out, a quarter of Tripoli was Jewish, and the city was home to 44 synagogues. When Israel was formed in 1948, most Libyan Jews opted to immigrate there. Colonel Qadhafi expelled the remaining Jews from the country in the 1970s.

Below: The prayer hall of a mosque is often well decorated.

26

Left: **These men are reading the Qur'an, the holy book of the Islamic faith.**

Islam has two major denominations: the Sunni and the Shiite schools. Libyans are mainly Sunni Muslims. All Muslims follow five tenets, or principles: they must pray five times a day; they must donate money to the poor; they must fast during the month of Ramadan; they must make a pilgrimage to the holiest Islamic city, Mecca in Saudi Arabia; and they must say the *shahada* (shah-HAH-dah), the prayer that says they believe there is no god but Allah and that Muhammad is Allah's prophet.

Religion in Daily Life

Islam exerts a strong influence on the daily lives of Libyans. The shari'ah code, which is a set of laws based on the Islamic principles in the Qur'an, forms the basis of Libya's legal system. Libyans pray five times a day; the men pray in mosques, while the women pray mainly at home. Friday is the main day of prayer for Muslims, and every Muslim goes to the mosque on this day, with men and women praying in separate areas.

Religion also forms a part of daily greetings and everyday speech. Libyans greet each other with the phrase "peace be with you," while the phrase "if Allah wills it" is usually added on to sentences that express hopes and desires, showing that Libyans leave all matters to the will of God, and faith is a central part of life.

BERBER AND TUAREG RELIGION

Berbers and Tuaregs follow Islam. Their religious practices, however, sometimes incorporate the belief in animism — the worship of spirits found in nature — and Christianity. The belief in magic and the sacred power of a particular site, as well as the role of holy men, who are venerated after their deaths, are important to these people.

Language and Literature

Arabic is the dominant language all over Libya, but in cities, English and Italian are also commonly spoken. The official language of Libya is Arabic, and it is used in government, education, and business. English is occasionally used in some government publications and is also taught in schools in Libya's major cities. Italian is also widely undesrtood in major cities. Berber and Tuareg communities in Libya speak their own language, called Tamazight, and its various dialects.

Literacy in Libya has improved over the last thirty years, due in part to the government's strong efforts to support education. Among the population aged 15 years and above, about 82.6 percent is considered literate. Women in this group have a literacy rate of 72 percent, while men have a literacy rate of 92.4 percent. Newspapers in Libya are controlled by the government. All newspapers are printed in Arabic, but some newspapers also have English editions. The official government news agency of Libya is Jana, short for the Jamahiriyah News Agency.

TAMAZIGHT

Tamazight, or Tamashek, is spoken by the Berber and Tuareg people. The language has many different dialects, but in Libya, the main dialects are Tawjilit, Tarquet, and Tanefusit.

Below: **Signs in Libya are often written in two languages, Arabic and English. Although Arabic is spoken throughout the Islamic world, each Islamic country uses the language differently. In Libya, for example, spoken Arabic includes many words from Italian and Tamazight.**

28

Bedouin Poetry

The classical literature of Libya is written in Arabic and includes Bedouin poetry. Bedouin poems have been passed on through the oral tradition and were only written down in the last hundred years. Bedouin poetry is not recited in the same manner as Western poetry. The poems are sung, sometimes accompanied by hand drums and hand claps to keep the rhythm. The audience also joins in the recitation, repeating important verses from the poem. One famous Bedouin poet in Libya is Abd al-Muttalab al-Jamaa'i. He was born in the 1820s and composed many poems. One of his better known poems is called *Arham booy khallani hawawi* and expresses the poet's immense joy and pride in Bedouin culture. Another famous poet, Haashim Bu al-Khattabiya, composed *Dialogue with a Well* in the middle of the twentieth century. In this poem, a man has a conversation with a well he used to visit in his youth. One of the most celebrated Libyan Bedouin poems is about the Al-Agaila concentration camp, in which many Libyans were interned during the country's Italian occupation. The poet, Sheikh Rajib Buhwaish al-Manfi, captures the cruel conditions of the camp in great detail.

THE GREEN BOOK

The Green Book (*below*) is a work of political literature written by Colonel Qadhafi in the mid-1970s. The book describes the philosophy behind Libya's government. Written in three parts, *The Green Book* describes an alternative society that is governed by *Jamahiriya*, or a "state of the masses."

Arts

Beautiful and Unique Architecture

The architecture of Libyan buildings is a highly visible aspect of Libya's rich artistic heritage. A variety of architectural styles and periods can be found throughout the country. The Tripolitania region contains the remains of Roman towns, such as Sabratha and Leptis Magna. Features of these towns include ruins of temples, forums, basilicas, villas, baths, circuses, and theaters. Greek and Roman ruins can also be found in Cyrenaica.

Islamic architecture is also very evident in Libya through its beautiful mosques. Mosque buildings are usually comprised of a large prayer hall, a minaret, and a series of domes that serve as part of the roof. Some older mosques incorporate pillars and columns, signs of Libya's Roman past.

The architecture of the Berber and Tuareg people also forms an important part of Libya's architectural heritage. Of the two, Berber architecture generally is the better known. The main

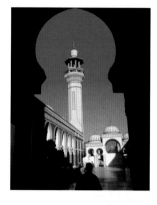

MAGNIFICENT MOSQUES

As befitting Libya's rich history, the country has a large number of beautiful mosques (*above*) that are built in a variety of architectural styles.
(*A Closer Look, page 62*)

THE RUINS OF LEPTIS MAGNA
The ruins at the ancient Roman city of Leptis Magna (*left*) provide a hint of the many splendid buildings that were built in Libya more than two thousand years ago.
(*A Closer Look, page 68*)

feature of Berber architecture is the *qasr* (KAH-ser), or "castle." These structures are found in the Jabel Nafusah area and date from the twelfth century. The qasr functions as both a fortified area as well as a place to store grain and other food such as olive oil. The storage areas of the qasr are carved out of its rock-and-gypsum structure and include rooms above and below the ground. Today, some qasr are still used as storage areas. The underground dwellings of some of the community living around the Jadu area are an example of Berber architecture. These homes are carved out of the earth and comprise a courtyard surrounded by rooms that are also carved out of rock.

Libya also has some beautiful examples of nineteenth- and twentieth-century city architecture, including official buildings, residences, and hotels. These buildings are designed in the neo-Moorish style, which combines elements of Arabic and Islamic architecture with Western styles. Contemporary Libyan buildings are made of glass, steel, and concrete and project a modern and international look.

Above: **Many houses in Libya are built with a central courtyard to provide the home with air and natural light. The homes of wealthy Libyans, such as this one in Tripoli, may even include a fountain feature.**

Music and Dance

Music and dance are part of Libya's rich traditions. Weddings and parties are the best times to experience Libyan music and dance. Some cities, such as Ghat, Ghadames, and Zouara, also hold festivals that showcase Libya's performing arts. The dances at these festivals portray scenes from daily life. Dancers are accompanied by musicians who sit in a circle playing drums and flutes. Special dances take place at weddings and holidays. At New Year festivities among the Tuareg people, for example, women play the *tende* (TEN-day), a drum, while singing songs about Tuareg heroes. The men, for their part, ride their camels in a circle around the women. The community also has various wedding dances that are performed during marriage celebrations.

Traditional Libyan musical forms include the *malouf* (muh-LOOF) and the *alaam* (AH-lah-mm). Malouf music is heard at weddings and involves groups of guests who sing religious and love poetry. The alaam involves two singers who sing to each other. Instruments used to perform traditional Libyan music include the *gheeta* (HEE-tah), which resembles the clarinet, and the *nay* (NAH-ee), which is a type of flute. Another instrument, the *zukra* (ZOO-krah), sounds like bagpipes.

Left: **Dressed in traditional costumes, these dancers also play the drums while they dance. The drums are used to provide rhythm.**

Left: Craftsmen in Libya are highly skilled, and even ordinary household items, such as these copper pots and trays, feature intricate designs.

ROCK ART

Images of people and animals carved on rocks and cave walls in many parts of the Libyan desert provide people today with a better understanding of life during ancient times.
(A Closer Look, page 66)

Handicrafts

The creativity of the Libyan people is illustrated through the country's varied handicrafts. Carpets, pottery, baskets, silver and gold jewelry, and textiles are popular with Libyans and tourists alike. Craft industries exist both in cities and in rural areas, with city crafts being more developed than those produced in the countryside. City craftsmen produce leather goods such as *belgha* (BEL-ha), or traditional shoes, as well as copper pots and trays and elaborate wooden marriage chests. Gharyan has a large pottery industry, while Ghadames produces bright leather shoes.

Carpets, pottery, and jewelry are often decorated with geometric patterns and shapes such as triangles, rectangles, dashes, dots, squares, and diamonds. Carpets and textiles can be extremely colorful, especially the traditional veils and clothes worn by Berber women. Silver jewelry is a trademark of Berber and Tuareg women, while Libyan jewelers in the cities produce ornate gold jewelry that is very popular for weddings.

CONTEMPORARY LIBYAN PAINTING

Recently, Libyan artists have been making their works more accessible through the Internet. Famous Libyan painters include Ali al-Abani; Aki Zwaik; Afaf al-Somali, a female painter; and Mohammad Zwawi, a cartoonist. These artists produce landscapes and more abstract works using different media, including oil paints, inks, and watercolors.

Leisure and Festivals

Libyans spend their leisure time relaxing with friends and family. Leisure activities in Libya are diverse and range from watching television to going on summer holidays, from attending football matches to playing board games, and from listening to the radio to attending theatrical performances and festivals.

Watching television is a popular pastime in Libya. Because many Libyan homes have satellite dishes, Libyans have the choice of watching national or international programs. The satellite channel Al-Fa'adiya al-Jamahiriya offers programs from parts of the Middle East as well as international programs dubbed in Arabic. Libya's three local television stations broadcast news programs in Arabic, English, and French. Libyans also listen to radio broadcasts, which run for more than seventeen hours a day.

Board Games and Card Games

Board and card games are also popular with Libyans, young and old. Card games include *romeeno* (roh-MEEN-noh), a version of gin rummy, and *shkubbah* (SHKOO-bah), a card game where players work in two pairs to see which pair can win the most number of cards. *Seeg* (SEEG), a traditional board game from the Libyan

Left: **If Libyan men have free time during the day, they may spend it with male friends and relatives. In the evenings and on weekends, when they are at home, they watch television or listen to the radio with their families.**

Left: Many Libyan families go on vacation in the summer. Some families even book villas in tourist villages for up to four months.

countryside, involves tossing a two-sided stick and moving pieces on a board resembling a checkerboard. The aim of the game is to move the pieces around the board without getting pushed back by obstacles or by the other players' pieces. The board game *kharbga* (KARB-gah) is similar to othello or reversi. Players try to capture as many of the opponent's game pieces as possible.

Many traditional games, particularly those in the countryside, are played with small stones, date pits, or palm pieces. Libyans enjoy playing board and card games at home; in tea shops, cafés, and restaurants; or in open courtyards and under palm trees at oases.

Tourist Villages

Libyans do not travel overseas very much due to government restrictions, but they certainly like traveling around Libya, especially in the summer. The government has built tourist villages in scenic locations around the country to cater to the domestic tourist market. These tourist villages consist of self-catered accommodations, restaurants, activity centers, game rooms, and sporting facilities, and cater to Libyan families with children. Tourist villages are found at Libya's famous beaches along the northern coast, as well as in the country's interior.

BEACHES

Libya has some of the most beautiful beaches on the North African coastline. Locals and tourists flock to the beaches, especially on weekends and in the summer. Many tourist villages are located near beaches, so families can spend their summer holidays by the sea.

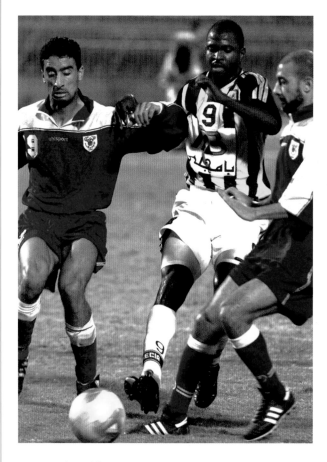

Football

Football, or soccer, is the main sporting activity as well as the main spectator sport in Libya. The sport is governed by the Libyan Football Federation, which was founded in 1962. A year after its founding, the Libyan Football Federation affiliated itself with the Fédération Internationale de Football Association (FIFA), which is the governing body of football at the international level. Within FIFA, Libya also belongs to the African regional football body called the Confédération Africaine de Football.

In Libya, local teams are organized into leagues, and the Libyan Football Federation organizes games between these teams. Well-known teams include the Al-Ahly, Al-Ittihad, and Al-Madina teams, all based in Tripoli. Benghazi-based football teams include the Al Tahaddy and Al Nasr. The Championship Cup and the Al-Fatah Cup, or Libyan Cup, are two important national competitions. Famous Libyan footballers include Jihad al-Muntasser; Tariq al-Taib, who plays for the Tunis Football Club; and Saadi Qadhafi, the son of Colonel Qadhafi.

Above left: **In January 2003, Libya competed in the first Arab Clubs' Competition held in Jeddah, Saudi Arabia. Libya's Nadr Karah (***left***) fights for the ball with Saudi Arabia's Hamza Idris (***center***) as teammate Adel Shatawi (***right***) moves in.** *Above right:* **In another game, Hamdi al-Marzouk of Tunisia (***left***) challenges Aravi Bin Yousek (***right***) of Libya for the ball.**

Saadi Qadhafi plays for the Al-Ittihad club, and in 2003, he was given the opportunity to train with the Italian football team Perugia.

Libya's national team takes part in international football competitions, including the African Cup of Nations competition, the Confédération Africaine de Football Cup, the Confédération Africaine de Football Champions League, and the African Cup of Football competitions. The Libyan Football Federation would like to host international football competitions and has placed bids to host events such as the 2005 World Youth Cup tournament and the 2010 FIFA World Cup competition.

Other Sports

Basketball, handball, and volleyball are played in the major sport centers in Tripoli and Benghazi. Sporting organizations include the Libyan National Olympic Committee, the Libyan Volleyball Federation, and the Libyan Tennis Federation. Organizations for karate and judo also exist to promote those sports. Women's sports include volleyball and table tennis. Camel and horse racing are popular in the countryside, especially in southern Libya. Horse racing and equestrian show jumping events also take place in Tripoli. Some Bedouin tribes may also hunt with salukis, which are graceful and swift desert greyhounds.

Above: **Many talented footballers, such as Saadi Qadhafi (*above*), are trying out for foreign teams. This trend has resulted in a small, but growing number of professional Libyan footballers who play outside the country.**

Left: **The Libyan government offers to host international events in order to boost its standing among other nations. In January 2003, stage six of the Paris-Dakar Motor Rally passed through Ghadames in northwestern Libya.**

Islamic Holidays

Libya celebrates both religious and civic holidays. The main religious holidays coincide with the major Islamic festivals of *Id al Saghir* (EED ahl suh-GEER) or *Eid al-Fitr* (ead al-FIT-er) and *Eid al-Adha* (ead al-AD-hah). Id al Saghir is preceded by the holy month of Ramadan during which all Muslims are expected to fast. Fasting takes place between sunrise and sundown, and no food or water is to be consumed during these hours. The day's fast is broken by *iftar* (if-TAR), a family meal with lots of sumptuous delicacies. After iftar, families go out for walks and shopping. More pious families will spend the evenings of Ramadan praying and reading the Qur'an.

Fasting goes on for one month and ends with a great festival at Id al Saghir. Women prepare elaborate meals days before the event, while people buy new clothes and gifts for friends, relatives, and children. Everybody dresses up in new clothes on the morning of Id al Saghir. Families visit mosques for morning prayers and come home to large meals with the extended family and friends. Id al Saghir is a fun time for children; they receive lots of presents and are taken to small fairs set up in town and city squares. In Tripoli, families throng the Green Square to have their photographs taken by photographers, who provide decorated

Left: **This group of Libyan men and boys in Ghadames gathers to pray before breaking the fast during the month of Ramadan.**

Left: **During the celebrations for Eid al-Adha, rams are slaughtered as a symbol of Abraham's promise.**

horses, thrones, and cars to make the photographs extra special. Celebrations last for several days, during which businesses and government offices are closed.

Eid al-Adha takes place two months after Id al Saghir. This festival celebrates the story of Abraham, who was willing to sacrifice his own son out of obedience to Allah. The Qur'an recounts that Allah was so pleased by Abraham's willingness to obey that He stopped Abraham from killing the boy and ordered that a ram be sacrificed instead. During this festival, families slaughter rams and roast them for a traditional meal. Other religious festivals include the Islamic New Year and Prophet Muhammad's birthday. The dates for these Islamic holidays change from year to year as they follow the lunar calendar.

Other National Holidays

Civic holidays in Libya include the Declaration of the People's Authority Day on March 2 and Revolution Day on September 1. The Declaration of the People's Authority Day is a holiday that celebrates the founding of the Jamahiriya in 1977. Rallies are held in major cities, and speeches are broadcast on the radio and on television. Revolution Day is the most important civic holiday in Libya. In Tripoli and Benghazi, military parades, big rallies, and speeches by Colonel Qadhafi also take place.

FESTIVALS FOR TOURISTS

In an effort to attract more tourists to Libya, the Libyan government has established a number of festivals for tourists at important cultural sites in the country. These festivals take place in cities such as Ghadames, Zouara, and Ghat. The festivals celebrate the customs and traditions of the people living in these respective areas. The Ghat Festival, for example, is a showcase of Tuareg culture.

Food

Libyan food is a mixture of Mediterranean and Middle Eastern cuisine. The Italian influence on cuisine is strong in cities along the coast, where various pizzas and pastas, especially macaroni, are quite popular. Traditional Libyan dishes are more widespread in the southern part of the country. Since most Libyans dine at home with their families, the real cuisine of the country cannot be sampled by simply going to restaurants and cafés, which tend to serve international fare.

Couscous, a traditional North African dish, is made from boiled cereals such as millet, wheat, or barley. Large pieces of meat such as mutton and chicken are served with couscous, and potatoes also form part of the dish. A typical Libyan bread is *bazin* (buh-ZEEN). This unleavened bread has a paste-like consistency and is made from barley, water, and salt. *Aish* (AH-yeesh) is similar to bazin but softer. Bazin and aish are eaten with the hands and can be served with soup and fish. Other types of

Left: A traditional Libyan favorite is spicy *shurba* (SHOOR-bah). Ingredients used to prepare this soup include lamb, oil, onions, tomatoes and tomato paste, lemon, pepper, and cinnamon.

unleavened breads or pancakes include *bseesa* (buh-SEE-sah) and *fitaat* (fuh-TAAT). Bseesa is bread made from seeds that are crushed and mixed with oil. This bread is usually eaten at breakfast, with some tea. Fitaat is a pancake made from a mixture of buckwheat, lentils, and mutton that is cooked in a sauce. The pancake is eaten by hand out of a communal dish and is a specialty from the Ghadames region. Another dish that has bread as one of its ingredients is *matruda* (ma-TROO-dah), a delicious dessert made with pieces of oven-baked bread mixed with milk, butter, dates, and honey.

Bureek (BOO-reek) are delicious Libyan turnovers that can be filled with all sorts of different stuffing, including meat, spinach, eggs, or potatoes. A favorite lamb dish is *tajeen* (ta-JIN), in which the lamb is delicately spiced with paprika and tomatoes. Tomatoes also help flavor *rishda* (REESH-dah), a dish of vermicelli noodles, chickpeas, and onions. Sheep's stomach is the main ingredient in *osbane* (ose-BAHN), which consists of a sheep's stomach stuffed with rice, herbs, kidneys, livers, and other meats. This stuffed stomach is boiled in a sauce or steamed.

Above: **Locally grown produce, such as dates, tomatoes, and lentils, are sold at marketplaces in Libya.**

41

A CLOSER LOOK AT LIBYA

Libya's historical heritage is vast. The country has spectacular Greek and Roman ruins in Cyrenaica and Tripolitania respectively. The indigenous Garamantian civilization, which controlled the Fezzan region of southern Libya for centuries, also has left remarkable archaeological sites, and the country is home to a rich collection of Ottoman and Islamic art and architecture as well. Tripoli and Benghazi, the two largest Libyan cities, are where modern and traditional ways of living intermingle — where ancient ruins meet modern buildings and where desert Bedouin, Berber, and Tuareg peoples mix

Opposite: **Leptis Magna is a designated World Heritage Site. This view shows the entrance to the ruins of the Severan basilica from the Severan Forum.**

with urban Libyans. Libya is also home to engineering marvels such as the Great Manmade River Project. One of the amazing feats of survival in the Sahara is how desert communities have been able to harness limited water supplies to grow lush gardens and plant agricultural fields. Two of Libya's most precious resources, oil and water, are found in abundant quantities under the Saharan sand. The challenge ahead for the country is how to use these resources wisely to benefit the future generations of Libyans.

Above: **Just like children in other parts of the world, these boys in the city of Murzuq hang out with friends after school.**

Ancient Cyrene

Of the five ancient Greek cities that once lay on the northeastern coast, the city of Cyrene is considered by many people to be the most beautiful. According to local legend, Cyrene was founded when the Greek god Apollo kidnapped a nymph named Cyrene and took her to the area. The Temple of Apollo, the ruins of which can still be seen in Cyrene, was built to commemorate Cyrene and her amazing physical strength. The legend says that she was an excellent hunter who could strangle lions with her bare hands.

The Golden Age of Cyrene

Archaeological and literary evidence of the founding of Cyrene dates back to the seventh century B.C., when Greek settlers from the Mediterranean island of Santorini landed on the northeastern Libyan coast. The fertile agricultural land of Cyrenaica soon attracted more settlers from Greece, and Cyrene prospered. The golden age of Cyrene came in about the fourth century B.C., when the city was considered among the richest

Below: **The ruins of this basilica in ancient Cyrene show the advances that the Romans achieved in building technology. These columns are a combination of marble and sandstone.**

Left: The sanctuary of Zeus in the ancient city of Cyrene was built on a hill.

Greek cities in the Mediterranean. Not only did the city have enormous agricultural wealth and strong trading relations with the rest of the Mediterranean, but it also had a reputation as one of the major centers of Greek learning and philosophy. The philosopher Aristippus founded the Cyrenaic school of philosophy, and the city also was home to Theodorus and Eratosthenes, two famous ancient Greek mathematicians.

The Agora

Today, the ruins of Cyrene attract Libyans and foreigners alike. The center of Cyrene was the Agora, which functioned like a forum in a Roman city. The Agora was the main public square of the city and housed a market and many important religious and civic buildings. The Agora was also the place where leaders made speeches. Ruins of structures that can still be seen in the Agora today include the Temple of the Octagonal Bases, the Tomb of Battus, and the Naval Monument. Built between the third century B.C. and the second century B.C., the Naval Monument features a beautiful marble statue of a woman and two dolphins.

AN ANCIENT MATHEMATICIAN

Born in Cyrene, Eratosthenes (276–194 B.C.) was the third librarian of the Library at Alexandria. His written works include *Platonicus*, which deals with the mathematical principles in Plato's philosophy, and *On Means*, which talks about geometry. Eratosthenes also made contributions to geography. He mapped the course of the Nile River to Khartoum and was also the first to suggest the correct reason for the annual flooding of the Nile; heavy rains closer to the southern source of the Nile caused flooding farther north in Egypt.

Benghazi

Benghazi is located in western Cyrenaica on the northeastern coast of Libya. Founded by Greek immigrants, the original site of the city lay south of modern-day Benghazi and was called Euhesperides, after the Greek mythical garden of Hesperides. The city is mentioned in writings dating from the sixth century B.C., although by the third century B.C., it was called Berenice, after the wife of Pharaoh Ptolemy III of Egypt. By this time, the city had shifted to its present site. Benghazi came under Roman control several centuries later and suffered severe damage when Vandals invaded the city in the fifth century A.D. The city attracted little attention for the next thousand years, until the fifteenth century when it took on the name Benghazi, after a Muslim holy man, Ibn Ghazi, who was said to have performed many philanthropic works. The Ottoman Turks took over the city in the sixteenth century and made it a center for tax collection for the region. Unhappy with the Ottoman's move, the city's traders

Below: **Many ancient structures in Benghazi were destroyed as a result of bombing during World War II, and modern buildings such as this one have been built to replace older structures.**

left, and the city's fortunes declined until the mid-nineteenth century. Benghazi later became a strategic Italian port during the Italian occupation of Libya in the twentieth century. During World War II, the city was bombed heavily by both Allied and Axis powers and almost totally destroyed. The oldest buildings in Benghazi now only date from the mid-twentieth century, despite the city's long history.

Above: **The heart of Benghazi's medina, or old town, the Souq Al-Jreed, the city's noisy and covered market. A typical North African market, the Souq Al-Jreed sells everything from food to fashion to electrical appliances. Another colorful and vibrant market is the Al-Funduq market, which sells vegetables.**

Arab and Italian Influences

Benghazi is a unique mixture of Arab, Italian, and African influences, reminding visitors that North Africa is indeed situated at the crossroads of the Mediterranean, Africa, and the Middle East. The Italian-style buildings of Benghazi include the cathedral, town hall, and the old Egyptian consulate. Many of these buildings are pastel colored and have windows with wooden shutters. Elegant arched doorways, grand pillars, and paved courtyards form part of the Italian artistic legacy, although many of the buildings are now in disrepair. The Islamic-style buildings include the mosques with beautiful domes and minarets, and the four- or five-story homes and shops that line the narrow streets of the medina, or old town, of Benghazi.

The Berber

The Berber call themselves Amazigh, and their language Tamazight. This language has some three hundred dialects. The Berber are an indigenous North African people and were living in the region before the arrival of Arab tribes from the Middle East in the seventh century A.D. The centuries of cultural mixing between Arab and Berber mean that most of Libya's population today is described as having both Arab and Berber heritage. The Berber are also found in other North African countries, including Algeria, Tunisia, Egypt, and Morocco. Pure Berber clans and families are still living in Libya today, especially in the Jabal Nafusah region and in certain districts of major Libyan cities.

Berber Culture in the Jabal Nafusah

Berber culture has survived in the highlands of the Jabal Nafusah mainly through isolation. The communities here are closely knit and still speak the Berber language. The people have also retained the distinct architecture of their homes and their special form of the Islamic religion.

Below: **One example of unique Berber architecture is this granary carved out of rock. Although the granary was built in the twelfth century, some of the storage rooms are still in use today.**

Today, many tourists visit Jabal Nafusah to experience the traditional lifestyle of the Berber communities and to view the unique Berber homes. These dwellings have been carved out of the ground or from sides of hills. The homes provide shelter from the harsh environment as well as security, as they are only partly visible from the outside. Living inside homes carved from rock and mud helps Berber families endure the cold winters and harsh summers of the region. Other types of dwellings, including mosques, granaries, and military fortresses, also have been carved out of rock. Some of these buildings are still in use today. The majority, however, are empty, as an increase in wealth has sent many families to newer accommodations on the plains surrounding the ancient hillside homes.

Qasr al-Haj

The village of Qasr al-Haj is home to one of the largest examples of Berber architecture in Libya, a fortified granary that is circular in shape and enclosed by rock. In the twelfth century, Sheikh Abu Jatla built this granary to store food from the surrounding region. The sheikh forced farmers to place part of their harvest inside the store so that the local community had stored grain in case there was a poor harvest or any other emergency. Surrounding the main courtyard are 114 storage rooms carved out of gypsum and rock. Each room is sealed with doors made of palm trunks.

Above: **Many Berber still lead a traditional lifestyle and make a living by selling their livestock in the market.**

Foggara: Traditional Water Management

The desert oases communities of the Sahara Desert are good examples of how people are able to survive in a hostile environment. The indigenous peoples of the North African deserts have been able to live in harmony with their environment for thousands of years. Over the centuries, oasis communities have developed a technique for water management and agriculture that has helped them grow their own food. A system of underground networks of canals has been used by desert communities in countries as diverse as Mongolia, Iran, Saudi Arabia, Algeria, and Libya. In Libya and Algeria, these canals are called *foggara* (FOR-ga-rah). Although this traditional method of water management has declined in Libya over the last few decades, some oases in the Fezzan region still use the foggara to supply their homes, gardens, and fields with water.

Left: **In the area outside Ghadames, lush oases gardens are irrigated by a unique canal system that is designed to minimize water wastage.**

Underground Canals

Foggara are underground canals that transport water and bring it to the surface of an oasis. These canals are made from mud, stone, clay, and straw, with palm trunks as reinforcement, and they run from higher to lower ground. The foggara system, therefore, only works if the oasis is situated in a valley and the source of the water is at higher ground, for example inside cliffs or plateaus above the oasis. The foggara transport water with the help of gravity, as they are inclined at a slight angle. The gradual slope of the canals means that water travels slowly and does not erode the walls of the canal. The water can be transported for quite a distance without evaporating, since the canals are underground. Wells are built at regular intervals along the canals. These wells allow people to repair and check on the state of the canals as well as the water flow.

Distributing the Water

Once the water arrives at the oasis via the foggara, it is distributed to various houses, gardens, and agricultural plots through a network of canals. Water distribution is often managed by the oasis water tribunal, a group of community leaders who decide which families and which gardens get water on which day. Based on their decisions, the openings in the canal are either left open or blocked off so that water can flow to the designated area.

Foxes and Antelope

The Fennec Fox

The fennec fox is the smallest animal of the fox and wild dog families. A furry creature with large ears, the fennec fox is found in the deserts of North Africa and the Arabian Peninsula. On average, the fennec fox grows up to 17 inches (43 cm) in length and can weigh between 2 and 3 pounds (0.9 to 1.3 kilograms).

The fennec fox protects itself from the harsh heat of the desert by burrowing into the sand and passing the daylight hours hidden away in its underground den. These dens can be as long as 31 feet (9.4 m) and as deep as 3 feet (90 cm) underground. The paws of the fennec fox are lined with fur, and this lining helps protect the animal when it is walking on hot sand.

The large ears of the fennec fox not only help the animal detect the sounds of its prey — mainly small rodents and insects — but also perform a vital cooling function. When the animal feels too hot, its body pumps its hot blood into the veins in its ears. Here, the blood spreads out over the surface area of the ears and is in very close contact with the outside air through the skin on the animal's ears. This contact with the air helps cool the blood, thereby preventing the fennec fox from overheating. The fennec fox can also survive with very little water and can obtain water by eating leaves, roots, and berries.

Desert Antelope

The sands of the Libyan Sahara are also home to various types of desert antelope, including the dorcas gazelle, the oryx, and the addax. One of the world's rarest animals, the addax has beautiful spiral-shaped horns and is the antelope that has best adapted to desert life. One of the largest mammals in the Sahara, the addax can weigh up to 275 pounds (125 kg). Despite its size, the addax hardly needs to drink water because it gets its moisture from eating whatever thorns, bushes, and desert plants it can find. The addax also gets water from dew that condenses on the ground. It has the ability to spot sparse vegetation even from a long way off.

The dorcas gazelle is another Saharan antelope that can survive without water for long periods of time. This animal mostly lives on the fringes of the Sahara, but it sometimes ventures into the desert. Dorcas gazelles have small horns and are known to be fast runners, reaching speeds of up to 60 miles (96 km) per hour. Nearly extinct in the wild, the oryx has beautiful backward-curved horns and can survive without water for months at a time.

Above: These addaxes have been raised in a zoo in Australia. The Werribee Open Range Zoo in the state of Victoria has a breeding program for addaxes, which are nearly extinct in their natural habitat in North Africa.

Opposite: Fennec foxes are nocturnal animals and often live in small family groups. They can make quick movements and jump high in the air.

The Garamantian Civilization

The empires of Greece, Rome, and Carthage were not the only powers to leave their mark on ancient Libya. The Garamantians, an important indigenous people, also established an empire, which was centered in Fezzan, in the southwestern part of Libya close to the Wadi al-Hayat (also called Wadi al-Ajal). A wadi is the bed or valley of a stream that is usually dry except during the rainy season. The Wadi al-Hayat in Fezzan is particularly rich in water resources, which lie just below the dry sand.

History

Archaeologists believe the Garamantians were the major power in southern Libya between 500 B.C. and 500 A.D., and anthropologists believe the Garamantians are the ancestors of the Tuareg people of present-day Libya. The ancient Greek and Roman writers described them as being fierce and warlike. The empire grew rich from the trade routes that passed through their territory and linked the Mediterranean Coast with sub-Saharan Africa.

Left: **Shown here is an artist's impression of an ancient Garamantian man living beside the river.**

Above: **Beautiful oases can be found along the route from Sabha to Germa.**

When the Roman Empire conquered Carthage in Tunisia in 147 B.C., its armies sought to destroy the Garamantian empire and take control of its lands. The Romans sent many expeditions to the Fezzan to try and conquer the Garamantes, but their efforts proved futile. Eventually, the Romans were able to force a military alliance with the Garamantians, but only after sending an army of some 20,000 Roman centurions. Roman influence on the empire, however, was not strong. Trade continued to be the main source of wealth for the Garamantians. By the fourth century A.D., Roman control was waning, paving the way for the conquest of the region in 655 by Islamic tribes from Tunisia.

Garama Today

Much archaeological excavation is in progress at the site of the Garamantian capital, Garama, near Germa. The modern town of Germa is one of the largest settlements of the Wadi al-Hayat. Some of the buildings being excavated in Garama include forts on the wadi floor, as well as cave dwellings in the sides and on the tops of the wadi walls. Excavations are also being done at burial sites that are in the rock walls of the wadi.

Ghadames

Situated 398 miles (640 km) southwest of Tripoli, Ghadames is listed as a World Heritage Site by the United Nations Educational, Scientific, and Cultural Organization (UNESCO) for its unique architecture, which has been preserved for centuries. The old town houses are the best examples of architecture that can withstand the Sahara's harsh climatic conditions. Most of Ghadames's people now live in new housing built away from the old town, but the old town still remains the main cultural focus of the area.

A Major Saharan Trading Town

Ghadames was a major oasis town that benefitted from the centuries-old trans-Saharan trade that brought goods from central Africa up to the Mediterranean and vice-versa. Ghadames produced few goods, but its merchants were shrewd businessmen who owned large numbers of camel caravans that criss-crossed the Sahara laden with many goods. The merchants rarely traveled themselves; they used agents stationed in all the major cities of the Sahara to do business on their behalf. The merchants traded goods such as ostrich plumes, gold, ivory, silver, precious stones, horses, dates, glass, paper, and linen. Some also traded slaves.

Left: **A series of low walls divides the roof terraces of buildings in Ghadames. Since the women of Ghadames were supposed to remain at home, these terraces provided a place where they could interact with their female friends and neighbors.**

Left: Buildings in Ghadames's old town are often constructed using local material, such as fired mud bricks and lime.

Unique Architecture

The present dwellings in the old town of Ghadames date from the twelfth century. The old town remains within the oasis and has beautifully cultivated gardens. The traditional architecture of Ghadames's old town is perfectly suited to the heat of the Sahara. Homes are made from fired mud bricks, lime, palm tree trunks, and palm leaves. The two-story-high square homes are simple and elegant. On the first floor, rooms surround a large central courtyard. Palm tree trunks covered with mud and palm fronds support the upper floors. Circular holes in the ceilings allow natural light to enter the homes, the insides of which are painted white in order to reflect the light to other areas in the house that do not receive direct light. The kitchens are situated on the roofs of the houses, which are connected to each other via terraces. The corners of the roof terraces have pointed features that are meant to scare away evil spirits. Women were in charge of decorating the homes, and decorations also consist of geometric red patterns.

The streets of old Ghadames are narrow to allow the shadows cast by the homes lining the streets to shield pedestrians from the harsh sun. Many streets and squares are also covered. Luxuriant gardens grown below street level, close to the source of the oasis, help keep Ghadames green and cool.

WELL OF THE MARE

Legend has it that Ghadames was founded when a group of travelers stopped for lunch in the desert. Later in their journey, they realized that they had left a cooking pot back at their lunch site. They returned to the site and reclaimed their pot. Just as they were about to leave, one of the horses impatiently stamped the ground with its hooves, and water immediately flowed out in the form of a spring. The new-found oasis was then named *Ain-al Faras*, or "Well of the Mare," as well as Ghadames, which is a combination of the word *ghad*, which means "lunch," and *ames*, which means "yesterday."

The Great Manmade River Project

Libya's mainly desert climate means that water is a scarce resource. Although the country's main cities are located on the Mediterranean coast, the Libyan government believes the country does not have enough water reserves to sustain future development. A growing population and increased migration to the cities, as well as problems such as desertification, mean that Libya needs a regular and reliable source of water. To achieve this, the government embarked on an ambitious water project called the Great Manmade River Project. This project aims to transport water that exists in large quantities beneath the Sahara Desert to other regions in Libya via large underground canals.

Stage by Stage

Called An-Nahr Sinai, the project is comprised of five stages. Stages one and two have already been built, and the final stage is expected to be completed in about ten years' time. The first stage transports underground water from the area near Tazerbo to the

Below: **The concrete canals used for the Great Manmade River Project measure over 2,485 miles (3,998 km) in length. Each section is about 13 feet (4 m) in diameter and will be laid underground at a depth of about 23 feet (7 m).**

coastal region between Benghazi and Sirte. Stage two of the project extracts water from underground reserves in Murzuq and transports it to the Tripolitania region. Stage three will tap the underground waters near Al Kufrah and connect it to the canals built in stage one of the project. Stages four and five of the Great Manmade River project will extend the pipes and canal networks to Tobruk in the east and connect the Tripolitania and Cyrenaica networks. Once the project is fully operational, it should be able to transport 7.8 million cubic yards (6 million cubic meters) of water a day to Libya's cities, farms, and industries.

Above: **Large volumes of freshwater lie beneath the sand dunes of the Sahara. The Great Manmade River project will bring some of this water to Libya's people.**

Challenges Ahead

Many scientists are worried that the water reserves under Libya's deserts could become depleted in a few decades, resulting in almost total loss of agriculture in oases that have survived for thousands of years. Northwestern Libya is already showing evidence of having less groundwater as a result of water extraction for the water canals. The first two stages of the project are also encountering problems, such as corrosion, which has caused the water flow to stop several times. The existing network is also not running at full capacity due to leakage. The project has cost more than U.S. $10 billion so far, and costs are expected to rise as the next stages of the project are constructed. It remains to be seen if the Great Manmade River Project is a success.

The Italian Occupation

From the mid-19th century onward, many European power were interested in acquiring African territories to boost their economies and international prestige. By the end of the 1880s, Italy had occupied Eritrea and southern Somalia. In 1911, Italy invaded what is now Libya, then controlled by the Ottoman Empire. The Italians formally gained Libya in a 1912 treaty.

Resistance to Italian Rule

Resistance to Italian rule was strong, especially in the first few years of the occupation. The Italians were able to establish strong control of the Tripolitania region by 1914. Fezzan and Cyrenaica, however, still experienced serious rebellions. These rebellions were mostly led by the Sanusiyah religious order. The Sanusiyah disliked foreign authority and had caused the Ottomans problems before the Italians arrived in 1911. The rebellions continued into the 1920s, when the Italians took more and more extreme measures to assert control over Libyan territory. Cyrenaica officially surrendered only in the mid-1920s, but rebellions carried on into the 1930s. The interior Fezzan region of Libya was not conquered until the mid 1930s.

Below: **Italy occupied Libya from 1911 to 1943. Italian dictator Benito Mussolini (*left*) waves to the Libyan crowd that came to greet him during his visit to the country in 1940.**

Left: During World War II, British prisoners of war captured at Tobruk, Libya, were sent to prison camps in Italy. Italian occupation of Libya ended when Allied forces defeated Axis forces in Libya in 1943.

Omar al-Mukhtar

The Libyan resistance to Italian rule only lessened with the capture of Omar al-Mukhtar, the leader of the Sanusiyah, who led the resistance through much of the 1920s and early 1930s. Al-Mukhtar was able to unite Libya's diverse nomadic tribes into an effective force that limited Italian control of much of Libya. Al-Mukhtar was captured by the Italians in 1931 and hanged. He was seventy-three years old and earned the nickname "Lion of the Desert" for his courage and sacrifice.

A Brutal Regime

In 1931, the Italians built a barbed-wire fence stretching from Bardia on the Mediterranean coast to Al Jaghbub, an oasis about 168 miles (270 km) from the coast. This fence successfully stopped supplies and guerilla reinforcements in Egypt from reaching the Libyan resistance. The Italians also ended civilian support for the resistance by moving entire villages of people into concentration camps. More than 100,000 people were moved to camps, and many of them died from starvation and disease. Overall, it is estimated that nearly half the population of Cyrenaica died during the Italian occupation, either from fighting or of disease and starvation. In July 1999, the Italian government formally apologized to Libya and offered U.S. $260 million as compensation for the suffering caused during the Italian occupation.

Above: Count Italo Balbo (1896–1940), an Italian aviator and the former Minister of Aviation in Italy, became the governor of Libya in 1933. In 1940, he was killed in Tobruk when his plane was brought down.

Magnificent Mosques

Libya boasts many beautiful mosques, which are places of worship for the Muslim community. It is believed that the first mosques evolved from the design of Prophet Muhammad's house. Today, the main areas of a mosque are the courtyard and the prayer hall. Inside the prayer hall are the *minbar* (MEHN-bar), a pulpit from which the sermon is delivered, and the *mihrab* (MUH-huh-rahb), the niche in the wall that indicates the direction of Mecca, Islam's holiest city. Prayer halls and minbar are often decorated with ceramic tiles, Arabic calligraphy, and detailed carvings of elegant geometric shapes. Another important part of the mosque is the minaret, which is a tower from which Islamic prayers are chanted over microphones.

Left: **Impressive new mosques, such as this one in Ghadames, boast marble pillars and towering minarets.**

Left: **Formerly the Roman Catholic cathedral in Tripoli, this church was converted into a mosque when large numbers of Italians left Libya in 1970.**

The Qaramanli Mosque

Officially called the Ahmad Pasha Qaramanli Mosque, this mosque has elaborate, carved woodwork in the prayer hall. These carvings depict plant motifs such as trees and flowers. Nearly thirty domes adorn the ceiling of the prayer hall, and each dome is decorated with these wooden carvings.

The Gurgi Mosque

The Gurgi Mosque was built in the early 1800s by Mustapha Gurgi. Although small in size, Gurgi's prayer hall is among the most beautiful of all of the prayer halls in Libya's mosques. It is decorated with ceramics, marble, and elaborate stone work.

Other Famous Mosques

Located in the medina, or old town, of Tripoli, the Othman Pasha Mosque also has an Islamic school, or *madrassa* (muh-DRAS-sah), attached to it. Beautiful Italian marble columns line the courtyard, which has a pool dating from the Roman era. The madrassa has been teaching students for over 350 years. Opposite the Othman Pasha Mosque is the Draghut Mosque, a sixteenth-century construction named after the pirate Draghut who ruled Tripoli between 1553 and 1565. Its prayer hall contains fifteen beautiful marble pillars and archways.

Oil: Libya's Gold

Oil is Libya's most valuable natural resource. It is so valuable that it is sometimes referred to as Libya's gold. The country is one of Africa's major oil producers and is North Africa's largest supplier of oil to the European Union. Oil was first discovered in Libya in 1959 near the Algerian border. After the discovery, Libyans as well as foreign oil explorers mapped oil fields in the Cyrenaica and Sirte regions. Foreign oil companies were the first to begin tapping Libya's oil reserves. Since that time, the Libyan oil industry has undergone significant changes. From 1969 onward, the industry was nationalized, or brought under government control. This move reduced the amount of foreign investment in the oil industry. Foreign involvement in Libya's oil industry was further reduced between 1992 and 1999, when the United Nations imposed sanctions on the country. Since the suspension of U.N. sanctions in 1999, Libya's oil industry has attracted much foreign investment. Libya's oil exports currently contribute between 75 and 90 percent of the country's total revenues. With the lifting of U.N. sanctions in September 2003, revenues from oil exports are expected to increase further.

Left: **Libya produces more than one million barrels of oil per day with some of it coming from the offshore Bouri oil field. Libyan oil is in high demand all over the world because it is of very high quality and contains few contaminants.**

Left: This oil flare is at a Libyan inland oil field. An oil flare is a flame produced by burning off waste gas. This waste gas is a by-product of drilling for oil. The Libyan government is attempting to attract foreign investment in the oil industry. This investment is needed to upgrade the country's oil-related infrastructure, such as drills, refineries, and oil pipelines.

National Oil Company

The main government company regulating the oil industry is the National Oil Company, with more than 30 subsidiary companies. From 1979 onward, the government has allowed the National Oil Company to make contracts with foreign oil companies in order to develop Libya's oil industry.

Main Oil Fields

Libya's oil reserves are found both on the mainland and offshore, along Libya's coast. The mainland oil fields, however, form the majority of the country's oil reserves. The main oil fields are found in the north, east, and west. The western oil fields include the Samah, Beida, Raguba, Dahra-Hofra, and Bahi oil fields. In the north are the oil fields of Defa-Wafa and Nasser. The Sarir, Messla, Gialo, Bu Attifel, Intisar, Nafoora-Augila, and Amal fields are found in eastern Libya. The main offshore oil field is the Bouri oil field located in the Gulf of Sirte. Currently, Libya's oil fields account for only about 25 percent of the country's total oil reserves. New oil fields are being planned in the Murzuq region, as well as in the Ghadames and Sirte regions. Oil exploration is also being conducted in the area around Al Kufrah and in other Cyrenaica regions.

Rock Art

Libya has some fine examples of ancient rock art. Dating back several thousands of years, this art has been carved or painted on stone walls and slabs in some of the most remote parts of the Libyan Sahara. No one knows for certain who painted the incredibly lifelike images of animals and people. Archaeologists speculate that they could be the work of the ancestors of the Tuareg or even the Garamantians. What is certain is that this art depicts the changing environment of the Sahara and gives scientists an idea of what the area looked like thousands of years ago, when the Sahara was teeming with wildlife and filled with lush vegetation. The main sites for rock art in Libya are at Jabal Acacus and Wadi Methkandoush, both in southwestern Libya.

Paintings and Petroglyphs

Archaeologists have classified Libyan rock art into paintings and carvings, or petroglyphs. Scholars think that people carved petroglyphs with a heavy, sharp stone, sometimes using another stone as a hammer to guide the sharp stone. First, they carved an outline and then added the details inside the outline. To paint pictures, they used animal feathers or hair as brushes.

Left: Ancient Libyans obtained the red paint used in most of their rock paintings by crushing and burning stones that have a high iron content. After painting, a varnish of egg white or animal fat was applied to preserve the painting.

Left: This engraving of a dying elephant engraving is at Wadi Methkandoush. Almost 7.5 miles (12 km) of rock art can be found at Wadi Methkandoush, making this site one of the richest concentrations of ancient rock art in the world.

Jabal Acacus

Jabal Acacus is listed as a World Heritage Site by UNESCO because of its rich collection of ancient rock art. The area has a collection of huge stone formations that rise out of the sand. Some of Libya's oldest art is painted or carved on these massive stone formations. The art here depicts animals such as cows, giraffes, elephants, panthers, and camels; some human figures; and even some letters of the ancient Tuareg alphabet. Some of the most beautiful paintings include hunting scenes that show human figures chasing animals with bows and arrows.

Wadi Methkandoush

Wadi Methkandoush has some amazing works of rock art. There are literally hundreds of carvings of animals in the site's sandstone rock formations. These figures include wild cattle, giraffes, hippopotamuses, elephants, ostriches, and rhinoceroses. Human figures are also present, including men with animal horns and masks, as well as women. Some of the animal carvings are very lifelike and anatomically precise. Others are more abstract, and certain features such as horns and tusks are emphasized.

The Ruins of Leptis Magna

Leptis Magna, a port city on the northwestern coast of Libya, is one of the best preserved Roman cities in the Mediterranean region. Leptis Magna has a collection of fine classical buildings that date from the first century B.C.. The city's design follows Roman town planning rules and includes large monuments. These structures have remained well preserved because shifting sand dunes had covered them until about the seventeenth century. Today, restoration, reconstruction, and conservation have helped continue to preserve these spectacular ruins.

The Arch of Septimius Severus

This arch was completed in 203 A.D. and commemorates the return of Roman emperor Septimius Severus to his birthplace, Leptis Magna. Indeed, Severus was instrumental in developing Leptis Magna into an important economic and strategic part of the

Below: **These ruins of the ancient market place show a row of Corinthian-style columns constructed from gray granite.**

Roman Empire. Severus also encouraged the construction of fine monuments and civic buildings in the city. The arch is comprised of three archways, with four detached columns at its front and back. Its core is made of limestone and is covered in marble. Carvings adorn the entire structure. The lower panels of the arch depict scenes from Severus's rule. Eagles, symbols of Roman imperial power, adorn the top of the arch. Carvings of crowns, palm branches, vines, and mythical figures symbolize the power of Septimius and his family. This public monument was a major landmark in Leptis Magna and a clear sign not only of Roman power but also of the region's important role in the empire.

The Severan Forum

The Severan Forum is at the center of Leptis Magna. Columns and archways flanked the sides of the rectangular space, and their ruins can still be seen today. Many of the arches and columns are adorned with Gorgon heads. The Gorgon was a mythical creature that had snakes for hair and whose glance could turn a human into stone. Other figures carved into the stonework include the Roman Goddess of Victory and sea nymphs.

THE THEATER OF LEPTIS MAGNA

Leptis Magna's theater is the second-largest surviving Roman theater in Africa. It is 230 feet (70 m) in diameter, and its stage consists of three circular areas surrounded by beautiful columns dating to the second century A.D. Sculptures of gods and heroes also formed a backdrop to the stage. Two statues still standing include those of the twins, Castor and Pollux, carved out of marble. Roman myth states that these twins were the illegitimate children of Zeus.

Tripoli

Tripoli, Libya's capital, is also its largest city, with a population of about 1. 5 million people. Tripoli was founded around 500 B.C. by the Phoenicians, and, over the next twenty-five hundred years, it was ruled by a succession of different civilizations or peoples, including the Nubians, Romans, Vandals, Byzantines, Aghlabids, Fatimids, Almohads, Hafsids, Spanish, Ottomans, and Italians.

The Medina of Tripoli

The oldest part of Tripoli is the medina, or old town, which was built on the original Roman site of the city. The only structure dating from Roman times and still standing in Tripoli is the Arch of Marcus Aurelius. Built in 163 A.D., the arch features marble facades and carved reliefs of Roman gods such as Minerva and Apollo. Close to the arch stands the best known of Tripoli's mosques, the early nineteenth-century Gurgi Mosque. Adding to the diverse architectural styles in the medina is the former French

Below: **Tripoli today may appear modern, but its rich history has resulted in a city that is both modern and ancient, with buildings and archaeological remains dating from different eras.**

Consulate built in 1630. Another diplomatic building worth seeing is the former British consulate, which now houses offices and an exhibition gallery. Close by is the restored Jewish School, which has an important collection of the city's archives. Traditional Libyan design and architecture can be seen along the narrow streets of the medina, where doorways are elaborately decorated with colorful paint and framed by beautiful archways.

An important part of the medina are the numerous markets, called souqs (also spelled "souks"), as well as hostels where merchants traditionally stayed when visiting the city for trade and commerce. Different souqs sell different items; the Souq al-Sagha, for example, specializes in jewels.

Above: **A huge variety of items are on sale in souqs. These items include handicrafts, pottery, clothes, spices, vegetables, fruits, meat, and electrical goods, such as blenders, radios, and telephones.**

Tripoli's Turkish baths

Two of Tripoli's older Turkish baths are found in the medina, the Hammam Dragut and the Hammam al-Halga. The Hammam Dragut is considered the more beautiful of the two and has been in operation since the sixteenth century. The public baths are open to men on certain days and to women on other days. The baths have several rooms, each for a different purpose, such as bathing, getting a massage, or cooling off.

The Tuareg

The Tuareg are a semi-nomadic people who live in North Africa and sub-Saharan Africa. An Islamic people, the Tuareg are believed to have descended from the Berber tribes of southwestern Libya. Today, the Tuareg are recognized as a distinct ethnic community in the countries they inhabit, including Niger, Mali, Algeria, Libya, and Burkina Faso. Estimates put the total number of Tuareg living in North Africa and Sub-Saharan Africa at around one million. In Libya, about 17,000 Tuareg live mainly around the oasis towns of Ghat, Ghadames, and Murzuq.

Languages, Names, and Words

The Tuareg speak dialects of Tamazight that vary according to where the Tuareg live. The name "Tuareg" is actually the name that outsiders use to identify the Tuareg. They refer to themselves as *Kel Tamashek*, which literally means "people who speak the Tamashek language." The Tuareg language is also called Tamashek. Another name the Tuareg use to identify themselves is *Imashaghen*, which means "the noble and the free" and refers to the Tuareg reputation for fierce independence. Tamashek has its own script, called Tifinagh, and many ancient rock art sites in Libya feature carvings of this ancient script.

Above: **Even though the Tuareg may dress in traditional attire, they have been influenced by modern technology such as mobile phones.**

Left: **A group of Tuareg men share a conversation with the Sahara's sand dunes in the backround.**

72

Tuareg Life

The Tuareg place great importance on family and tribal ties. Most extended families live together in the same collection of tents or compounds. This practice is even kept by Tuareg who have settled in villages and cities. Women hold a high place in Tuareg society; they own the tents and compounds in which the family lives as well as any animals that belong to the family. Trade is done exclusively by men, but a woman can take part indirectly by sending her camels with a male relative. Women harvest crops, while men are in charge of planting and irrigating the crops. Women may own gardens and date palms and can pass on their property to female relatives and daughters. In fact, the clan to which a Tuareg belongs is determined by the mother's side of the family, while the father's clan determines the kind of work a Tuareg does. Trading is carried out mainly by Tuareg of noble birth, while herding and other domestic work is performed by people lower down the social ladder. Although they are an Islamic people, the Tuareg men, rather than the women, are traditionally required to wear a veil. The deep indigo turban and veil of the Tuareg men is instantly recognizable in the desert.

Above: **The Tuareg living in rural areas still follow traditional customs. Marriage usually takes place within the same social status, although this is less common among Tuaregs living in cities.**

RELATIONS WITH NORTH AMERICA

Libya's relations with the United States in particular, and with the Western world in general, have traditionally been characterized by aggression and violence. Media reports in Western countries have also portrayed Libya as a sponsor of terrorism worldwide. This situation has existed since Colonel Mu'ammar al-Qadhafi came to power in Libya in 1969. Recently, however, relations between the Libyan government and some Western governments, such as the United Kingdom and Canada, have improved slightly.

Opposite: **Libya and the United States enjoyed a period of friendship between 1951 and 1969. The United States established an embassy in Libya and U.S. Air Force men stationed in the country even put on rodeo shows for the locals.**

Institutes of research and diplomacy, as well as business organizations located in North America and Europe are trying to establish peaceful ties between the West and Libya. Libyans living outside of Libya, particularly those living in the United States, also have a role in trying to build people-to-people links, even if no relations exist at the governmental level. Officially, however, the United States continues to impose economic sanctions on Libya because the U.S. government believes Libya still poses a threat to world peace. It is hoped that Libya and the United States can one day enjoy friendly relations.

Above: **In the late 1980s, Libya was tied to a series of terrorist attacks against the United States and other nations. This situation led the United States to station an aircraft carrier off the Libyan coast from which military operations were launched.**

The Pirates of the Barbary Coast

Relations between the United States and leaders of the Libyan region stretch back more than two hundred years to a clash over piracy issues along the Mediterranean coast of North Africa. Piracy along this stretch of the coast was a serious problem from the sixteenth century onward, when the Ottoman leader Barbarossa, who controlled Algeria and Tunisia, used piracy to boost his political power. Barbarossa's name gave rise to the nickname "Barbary Coast," which came to describe the states of Tripoli, Tunis, Morocco, and Algiers until the nineteenth century.

The pirate leaders of these states operated in a simple way; soldiers had to pay up, or they would be killed or taken hostage. Governments that owned the ships would pay huge sums of money to the pirate leaders to avoid attack. Only ships from countries that had paid money, called tribute, were allowed to safely sail along the coast.

Before U.S. independence in the late eighteenth century, American ships in the Mediterranean coast were protected from piracy because the British government had been paying tribute to the Barbary pirates. Once the United States became a sovereign nation, it was required to pay tribute on its own behalf. Initially, the country paid up. In 1801, however, when Thomas Jefferson

Below: **The pirates operating in the Mediterranean Sea grew rich from the protection money they collected from passing ships. This illustration from the early nineteenth century shows the U.S. Navy attacking the pirates.**

became president of the United States, Jefferson decided not to pay the tribute. The pasha, or ruler, of Tripoli responded by declaring war on the United States. Over the next fifteen years, the United States sent military frigates and soldiers to the Mediterranean to fight the Barbary pirates. American naval ships bombed Tripoli several times. In 1815, after victories by the U.S. Navy against the pirates, a treaty was signed between the United States and the states of the Barbary Coast ending all future payment of tribute. This episode of U.S.-Libyan relations is commemorated in lyrics from the official hymn of the U.S. Marines, which begins "From the halls of Montezuma to the shores of Tripoli."

Above: **The people of Benghazi cheer as the Italians formally surrender to British authorities after being captured by British and Australian forces during World War II.**

World War II

Following the contact with what is now Libya in the late eighteenth and early nineteenth centuries, the United States did not have any major involvement with North Africa until World War II, in the mid-twentieth century. U.S. forces, commanded by General Dwight E. Eisenhower, fought German and Italian troops in Tunisia, Morocco, and Algeria. British, French, and Australian soldiers were active in Libya.

Libyan Independence

Following the end of World War II, the United States supported the United Nations resolution calling for Libyan independence in 1951. By 1954, both countries had full-fledged embassies operating on each other's soil.

The Qadhafi Era

Relations between Libya and the United States deteriorated when Colonel Mu'ammar al-Qadhafi seized power in Libya by means of a coup in 1969. The United States believed Qadhafi's foreign policy was aimed at supporting terrorism and creating instability in various African and Middle Eastern countries. The Qadhafi regime of the 1970s and 1980s donated large amounts of money to terrorist groups such as the Popular Front for the Liberation of Palestine, the Irish Republican Army, the Japanese Red Army, and the Tupac Amaru Revolutionary Movement in Peru. Qadhafi was also linked to the massacre of Israeli athletes at the Munich Olympic Games in 1972 as well as the kidnapping of ministers attending the conference of the Organization of Petroleum Exporting Countries (OPEC) in Vienna in 1975.

By the mid-1970s, the United States had already withdrawn its ambassador from Tripoli and had established restrictions on the exporting of military equipment and civilian aircraft into

Below: **At the 1972 Munich Olympic Games, the Olympic flag flies at half-mast during the memorial service for the Israeli athletes who were killed by terrorists.**

Libya. In December 1979, a mob of Libyans attacked the U.S. Embassy in Tripoli and set fire to it. In response, the United States withdrew its embassy staff and closed the embassy. The U.S. government further declared Libya a state sponsor of terrorism.

Above: **U.S. president Ronald Reagan (***left***) and his aides listen as Chief of Staff to the Air Force General Charles Gabriel (***standing***) briefs them on the results of bombing in Libya in 1986.**

Expulsions and Air Raids

Relations between the two countries reached an all-time low in the 1980s, during which the Qadhafi regime was linked to terrorist attacks against the United States and other European countries. In 1981, the United States closed the Libyan Embassy in Washington, D.C., and expelled Libyan diplomats. That same year, two Libyan fighter planes attacked U.S. aircraft that were participating in a military exercise over the part of the Mediterranean Sea claimed by Libya. The U.S. aircraft shot down the two Libyan planes. The U.S. State Department also stopped issuing passports for travel by U.S. citizens to Libya and advised all American citizens in Libya to leave. By the mid-1980s, the U.S. government had banned direct import and export of all goods, including oil, between Libya and the United States.

An Explosion in Germany

In early April 1986, a bomb exploded in a German discotheque. The attack killed three people, including two U.S. soldiers, and injured over two hundred others. The U.S. government believed the Libyan government was involved in the bomb plot. The United States therefore ordered air strikes against targets in Tripoli and Benghazi later that month. In retaliation, the Libyan government contacted terrorist groups in the Middle East that had been kidnapping U.S. citizens in Lebanon. Through payment, the Libyan government was able to secure one kidnap victim, a 62-year-old librarian at the American University of Beirut, and had him executed.

The Lockerbie Incident

In December 1988, an airplane belonging to U.S. airliner Pan Am crashed in Lockerbie, a town in Scotland, killing all 259 passengers, as well as 11 people on the ground. The aircraft was en route from London to New York. Most of the passengers were U.S. citizens. Investigations revealed that the cause of the disaster was a bomb that had exploded in midair.

Terror in the Skies Again

Less than a year later, a plane belonging to French airliner UTA crashed in Niger while en route from the Republic of Congo to France. This crash killed all 171 passengers on board. Investigators found that a bomb was the cause of the crash and that both the Pan Am and UTA bomb plots involved agents of the Libyan government. In 1991, prosecutors in the United Kingdom and the United States issued arrest warrants against two Libyan suspects who were working as Libyan intelligence officers. French courts also issued warrants against six Libyans believed to be involved in the UTA crash. Later that year, the British, French, and U.S. governments issued a statement to the Libyan government demanding that all the suspects be handed over for trial. Libya refused, however, saying that it would try the suspects itself.

Above: **Libyan Al-Amin Khalifa Fhimah, who was suspected to be one of the two men behind the 1988 bombing of a Pan Am flight, arrives in the Netherlands in 1999 to stand trial.**

United Nations Sanctions

In response to Libya's refusal to hand over the suspects, the United Nations Security Council passed a resolution in 1992 that banned arms shipments to Libya. Airplanes were also prohibited from flying into, out of, and over Libya. In 1993, the Security Council froze Libyan funds and commercial assets in other countries and banned the export to Libya of equipment for the country's oil refining and transportation industries. Most of the U.N. sanctions were suspended in 1999, however, when Libya agreed to hand over the Libyan suspects for trial in the Netherlands. United Nations sanctions against Libya were finally lifted in September 2003. Nevertheless, U.S.-imposed sanctions against Libya remain in place.

Below: **Wreckage from the Pan Am aircraft that exploded over Lockerbie, Scotland, in 1988 was strewn around the town.**

The Iran and Libya Sanctions Act

The 1996 Iran and Libya Sanctions Act was passed by the U.S. government to tighten existing economic sanctions on Libya and Iran, another country that the United States deems as being a terrorist threat. Under the act, the United States places sanctions on non-U.S. companies that invested more than U.S. $40 million in Libyan industries. Non-U.S. companies that trade with Libya in arms, certain oil equipment, and civil aviation services can also be sanctioned. The act forbids U.S. companies from performing any commerce, trade, or financial activities with Libya. In 2001, the act was renewed for a further five years, but the amount that can be invested in Libya was reduced to U.S. $20 million.

A Recent Thaw in Relations?

Some politicians and academics are predicting an improvement in relations between Libya and the United States, especially with the lifting of United Nations sanctions on Libya in 2003. They believe Libya is showing less and less signs of funding terrorist organizations around the world. Colonel Qadhafi has also shown that he is willing to embark on positive relations with Western governments. On the other hand, after the terrorist attacks on the United States in 2001 and the overthrow of Saddam Hussein in

Left: **Libyans have started to make their mark in world affairs. Najat Al-Hajjaji (*right*) was elected president of the United Nations Human Rights Commission on January 20, 2003. Here, she shakes hands with French Foreign Minister Dominique de Villepin.**

Left: President John F. Kennedy (*center*) of the United States stands with Crown Prince Hasan al-Rida al-Sanusi of Libya (*right*) during the prince's lunch visit to the White House, in Washington, D.C., in 1962.

Iraq in 2003, others feel that terrorism is an increasing threat and that the Libyan government has yet to fully distance itself from terrorist activities. Libya, however, did provide the United States with information after the 2001 attacks about terrorist groups linked to Al-Qaeda. Another sign of an improving situation came in April 2003, when the Libyan foreign minister stated that Libya had accepted responsibility for the 1988 Pan Am bombing and had set up a fund to compensate families of the victims.

While relations at the governmental level may be stagnant, many Western-based, nongovernmental and academic institutions are seeking to establish more dialogue between Libya and the United States. One such organization is the Middle East Institute, based in Washington, D.C. This institute seeks to promote an understanding between the United States and countries in the Middle East. In 2002, an expert in U.S.–Libyan relations, Ronald Bruce St. John, gave a talk on the subject at the institute's premises.

The Libyan American Friendship Association is another private organization that seeks to promote positive relations between Libya and the United States. The association seeks to hold dialogues between U.S. and Libyan academics, businesspeople, and politicians in order to find ways to improve U.S.–Libyan relations. Issues that the association seeks to address include ways of lifting the U.S. sanctions against Libya and promoting private business collaboration between the two countries.

THE ATLANTIC COUNCIL

Founded in 1961 in Washington, D.C., the Atlantic Council of the United States is a nongovernmental organization that seeks to promote positive relations between the United States and other countries. Under its Program on International Security, the council initiated a one-year study into U.S.–Libyan relations. The report, entitled *U.S.–Libyan Relations: Toward Cautious Reengagement*, was published in April 2003. It deals with a wide range of U.S.–Libya issues, including terrorism, oil, security, human rights, and weapons of mass destruction. The report encourages the United States government to change its attitude toward Libya and improve relations between the two nations.

The Tibra Foundation

The Tibra Foundation is a U.S.-based charity headquartered in Westerville, Ohio. The foundation seeks to promote the lives of Libyan women living in Libya and abroad. As part of its desire to showcase women's achievements, the organization started the Tibra Awards, which are given to Libyan women who have excelled in their fields. The awards also aim to encourage women to become future leaders of the Libyan community within Libya and in the United States. The Tibra Foundation has highlighted the lives of many ordinary Libyan-Americans who have contributed a great deal to their respective communities. These women include Iya Khalil, a research scientist who co-founded a New York-based company that does cancer research, and Fayruz Benyousef, who was born in Tripoli and now is a member of the Austin Ballet, a dance company based in Texas.

Libyan-Americans

Many Libyans live in the United States, through immigration or as children of Libyan parents. One famous Libyan-American is poet Khaled Mattawa, who was born in Benghazi, Libya. He emigrated to the United States in 1979 and is a professor of English and creative writing at California State University. Much of Mattawa's poetry and prose speaks of his experiences growing up in Libya.

Left: American citizen Tecca Zendrik, who holds the title "Miss Net USA," took part in the Miss Net World beauty pageant in Tripoli in November 2002. Two months later, she was awarded Libyan citizenship and appointed as the country's honorary consul to Washington.

Left: Canada and the United Kingdom both enjoy official diplomatic ties with Libya. In 2001, Her Majesty Queen Elizabeth II (*left*), who is also the chief of state of Canada, met with Mohamed Abdul Qasim Al-Zawi (*right*), the first Libyan ambassador to the United Kingdom in seventeen years.

Relations Between Canada and Libya

Unlike relations between the United States and Libya, official relations between Canada and Libya do exist. Canada established relations with Libya in 1968. In 1986, however, Canada imposed sanctions on Libya, after terrorist attacks that were linked to Libya took place in Europe. Relations between the two countries resumed after the United Nations suspended sanctions on Libya in 1999. The Canadian ambassador to Tunisia currently also serves as the ambassador to Libya. Libya's embassy in Canada is located in Ottawa, the country's capital city.

In January 2001, David Kilgour, the Canadian Secretary of State for Latin America and Africa, visited Libya and inaugurated the new Canadian Embassy in Tripoli. This event marked the first time a Canadian minister had ever visited Libya. The Canadian government estimates that about one thousand Canadians currently live and work in Libya.

Canada and Libya also enjoy trade relations. Canada exports agricultural products, such as wheat and dairy products, and machinery to Libya. Canada's exports to Libya amounted to CAN $20 million in 2001. Canadian oil companies are interested in developing Libya's oil industry. Trade, however, is currently mostly one-way, as Canada imports very few goods from Libya.

CANADA–LIBYA BUSINESS TIES

The Canada–Libya Chamber of Commerce and Industry, based in Ottawa, Canada, is a business association that seeks to promote commercial, economic, industrial, and financial ties between Canada and Libya. The chamber also acts as an advisor to government agencies in Canada on Canada–Libya trading ties and promotes Canadian businesses within Libya. The chamber has participated in the 2002 and 2003 Tripoli International Fairs, which are aimed at promoting foreign investment in Libya's many industries.

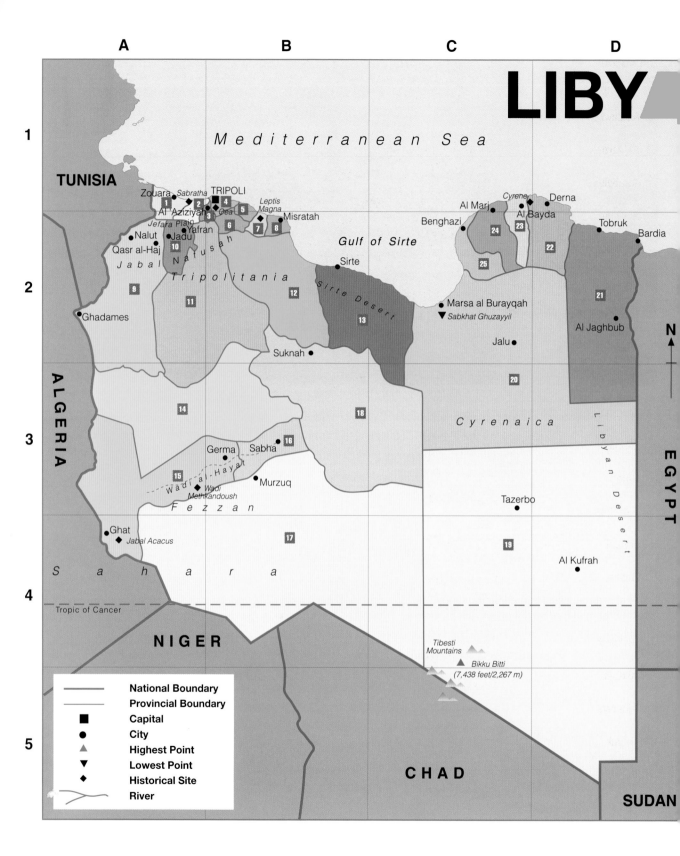

LIBY

Map Labels

Mediterranean Sea

TUNISIA

Zouara *Sabratha* **TRIPOLI**
Al Aziziyah *Oea*
Yafran
Jefara Plain
Nalut Jadu
Qasr al-Haj
Jabal Nafusah
Tripolitania
Leptis Magna
Misratah

Jabal Acacus

Al Marj *Cyrene* Derna
Benghazi Al Bayda
Tobruk
Bardia

Gulf of Sirte

Sirte

Sirte Desert

Marsa al Burayqah
Sabkhat Ghuzayyil

Al Jaghbub

Jalu

Ghadames

Suknah

Cyrenaica

Libyan Desert

N

ALGERIA

EGYPT

Germa Sabha
Wadi al-Hayat
Wadi Methkandoush
Murzuq
Fezzan

Tazerbo

Ghat
Jabal Acacus

Al Kufrah

Sahara

Tropic of Cancer

NIGER

Tibesti Mountains
▲ Bikku Bitti
(7,438 feet/2,267 m)

CHAD

SUDAN

Map Numbers
1, 2, 3, 4, 5, 6, 7, 8, 10, 11, 12, 13, 14, 15, 16, 17, 18, 19, 20, 21, 22, 23, 24, 25, 8

Legend

	National Boundary
	Provincial Boundary
■	Capital
●	City
▲	Highest Point
▼	Lowest Point
◆	Historical Site
∿	River

BALADIYAH

1 An Nuqat Al Khams

2 Az Zawiyah

3 Al 'Aziziyah

4 Tarabulus

5 Al Khums

6 Tarhunah

7 Zlitan

8 Misratah

9 Ghadames

10 Yafran

11 Gharyan

12 Sawfajun

13 Sirte

14 Ash Shati

15 Awbari

16 Sabha

17 Murzuq

18 Al Jufrah

19 Al Kufrah

20 Ajdabiya

21 Tobruk

22 Derna

23 Al Jabal Al Akhdar

24 Al Fatih

25 Benghazi

Above: In a dry desert, an oasis provides a source of drinking water and also supports the growth of plants.

Al Aziziyah B1
Al Bayda C1
Al Jaghbub D2
Al Kufrah D4
Al Marj C1
Algeria A2–A4

Bardia D2
Benghazi C2
Bikku Bitti C4

Chad B4–D5
Cyrenaica C1–D3
Cyrene C1

Derna D1

Egypt D2–D4

Fezzan A3–B4

Germa/Garama B3
Ghadames A2
Ghat A3
Gulf of Sirte B2–C2

Jabal Acacus A4
Jabal Nafusah A2–B2
Jadu B2
Jalu C2
Jefara Plain A2

Leptis Magna B2
Libyan Desert D3–D4

Marsa al Burayqah C2
Mediterranean Sea A1–D1
Misratah B2
Murzuq B3

Nalut A2
Niger A5–B5

Oea B1

Qasr-al Haj A2

Sabha B3
Sabkhat Ghuzayyil C2
Sabratha A1
Sahara Desert A3–D5
Sirte B2

Sirte Desert B2–C2
Sudan D5
Suknah B2

Tazerbo C3
Tibesti Mountains C4
Tobruk D2
Tripoli B1
Tripolitania A1–B2
Tunisia A1–A2

Wadi al-Hayat A3–B3
Wadi Methkandoush A4

Yafran A2

Zouara A1

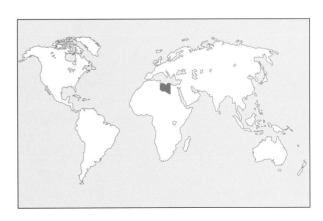

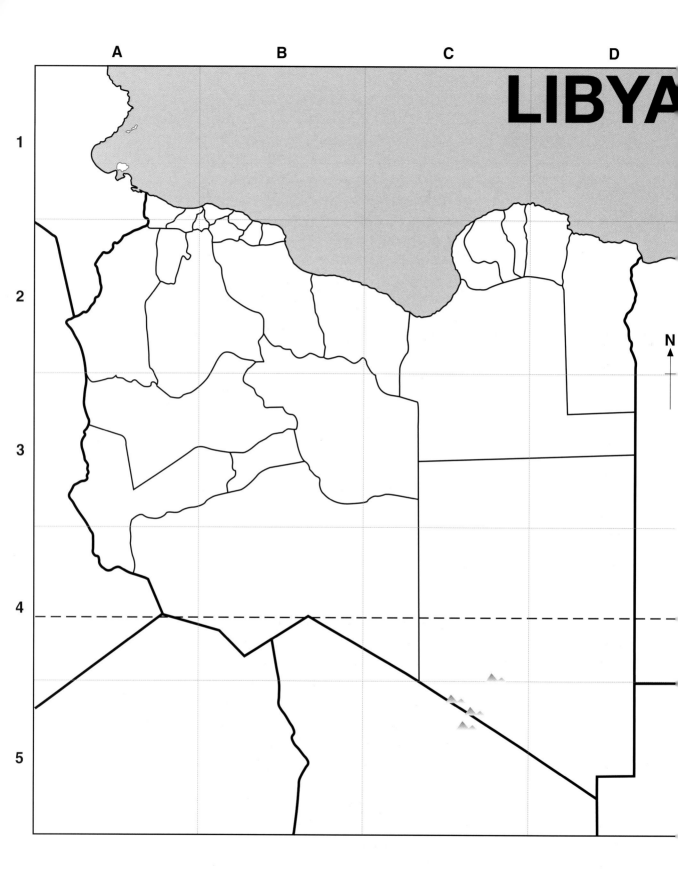

LIBYA

N

Above: **Although the climate makes it difficult for plants and animals to survive in the deserts of Fezzan, it is still an area of great natural beauty.**

How Is Your Geography?

Learning to identify the main geographical areas and points of a country can be challenging. Although it may seem difficult at first to memorize the locations and spellings of major cities or the names of mountain ranges, rivers, deserts, lakes, and other prominent physical features, the end result of this effort can be very rewarding. Places you previously did not know existed will suddenly come to life when referred to in world news, whether in newspapers, television reports, other books and reference sources, or on the Internet. This knowledge will make you feel a bit closer to the rest of the world, with its fascinating variety of cultures and physical geography.

This map can be duplicated for use in a classroom. (PLEASE DO NOT WRITE IN THIS BOOK!) Students can then fill in any requested information on their individual map copies. The student can also make a copy of the map and use it as a study tool to practice indentifying place names and geographical features on his or her own.

Libya at a Glance

Official Name   Socialist People's Libyan Arab Jamahiriya

Capital   Tripoli

Official Language   Arabic

Official Religion   Islam

Population   5,499,074 (July 2003 estimate)

Land Area   679,182 square miles (1,759,081 square km)

Highest Point   Bikku Bitti 7,438 feet (2,267 m)

Lowest Point   Sabkhat Ghuzayyil 154 feet (47 m) below sea level

Coastline   1,110 miles (1,785)

Major Cities   Tripoli, Benghazi, Misratah, Sabha

Major Holidays   Declaration of the People's Authority Day (March 2)

Evacuation Day (March 28, June 11, October 7)

Revolution Day (September 1)

Day of Mourning (October 26)

Famous Leaders   Septimius Severus (145–211)

Ahmad Qaramanli (r.1711–1845)

Omar al-Mukhtar (1862–1931)

Mu'ammar al-Qadhafi (1942–)

National Anthem   *Allahu Akbar*

Exports   Crude oil, refined petroleum products

Imports   Machinery, transportation equipment, food, manufactured goods

Export Partners   Italy, Germany, Spain, Turkey, France, Switzerland, Tunisia

Import Partners   Italy, Germany, United Kingdom, Tunisia, France, South Korea

Currency   Libyan Dinar (LYD 1.22 = U.S. $1 as of July 2003)

 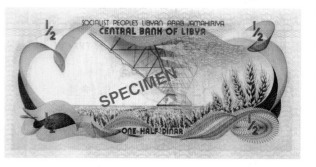

Opposite: **The ancient city of Leptis Magna was designated a World Heritage Site by UNESCO in 1982. These ruins in the forum area give an indication of the amazing structures that were once stood here.**

Glossary

Arabic Vocabulary

Aish (AH-yeesh): a Libyan bread made from barely, water, and salt.

alaam (AH-lah-mm): a traditional Libyan musical form where two performers sing to each other.

baladiyat (bah-lah-DEE-yaht): a unit of government the size of a municipality.

bayt (BAIT): the family; the smallest unit of a clan.

bazin (buh-ZEEN): a Libyan bread similar to Aish but with a firmer texture.

belgha (BEL-ha): traditional leather shoes;

bey (BAY): the title given to an official in charge of the Turkish province of Libya during Ottoman rule.

bseesa (buh-SEE-sah): bread made from crushed seeds and mixed with oil.

bureek (BOO-reek): a Libyan pastry filled with meat, spinach, eggs, or potatoes.

Eid al-Adha (ead al-AD-hah): a festival celebrating the tale of Abraham who was willing to sacrifice his son to Allah.

fitaat (fuh-TAAT): a pancake made from buckwheat, lentils, and mutton.

foggara (FOR-ga-rah): a system of underground water canals at an oasis.

gheeta (HEE-tah): a Libyan musical instrument resembling the clarinet.

Id al Saghir (EED ahl suh-GEER): also called *Eid al-Fitr* (ead al-FIT-er); an Islamic holiday after the fasting month.

iftar (if-TAR): a meal eaten to break a fast.

kharbga (KARB-gah): a board game where players try to capture as many of the opponent's game pieces as possible.

leff (LEEF): a grouping of clans through marriage or by region.

madrassa (muh-DRAS-sah): a school where the focus is on Islamic education.

malouf (muh-LOOF): a Libyan musical form heard at weddings when guests sing religious or romantic poetry.

matruda (ma-TROO-dah): a dessert of oven-baked bread mixed with milk, butter, dates, and honey.

mihrab (MUH-huh-rahb): the niche in the wall of a mosque showing the direction of Mecca

minbar (MEHN-bar): a pulpit in a mosque from which the sermon is delivered.

nay (NAH-ee): a Libyan musical instrument shaped like a flute.

osbane (ose-BAHN): steamed or boiled sheep's stomach stuffed with rice, herbs, kidneys, livers, and other meats.

qabilhah (kay-BIL-lah): a clan of people descended from a single ancestor.

qasr (KAH-ser): literally meaning "castle," a cave like structure dug out of the rock by the Berber and used for storage.

rishda (REESH-dah): vermicelli cooked with chick-peas, onions, and tomatoes.

romeeno (roh-MEEN-noh): a version of gin rummy played in Libya.

seeg (SEEG): a traditional Libyan board game resembling checkers.

shahada (shah-HAH-dah): the Islamic prayer stating that Muslims believe in only one god called Allah and that Muhammad is Allah's prophet.

shari'ah (sha-REE-yah): Islamic law.

sheikh (SHAKE): the head of a clan.

shkubbah (SHKOO-bah): a card game where players pair up to try and win the most number of cards.

shurba (SHOOR-bah): a spicy Libyan stew cooked with lamb, oil, onions, tomatoes, lemon, pepper, and cinnamon.

tajeen (ta-JIN): a spicy meat stew, usually containing lamb.

tende (TEN-day): a drum played by Tuareg women to accompany songs sung about local heroes.

zukra (ZOO-krah): a Libyan musical instrument that sounds like bagpipes.

English Vocabulary

allegedly: supposedly; asserted to be true.

alliance: a formal agreement between two or more countries to cooperate for specific purposes.

animism: the belief that natural items have souls.

assassination: the murder of someone, often a political leader, in a sudden, violent attack.

bluff: a hill with a broad steep face.

chameleon: a lizard that can change color to blend into its surroundings.

counterparts: a person who performs the same function as another but in a different country or organization.

deposed: removed from political office.

desertification: the processes by which an area by a desert.

domesticated: describing a once wild animal that has been tamed, either as a pet or a work animal, as a result of being in close association with humans.

enacted: brought about or put into place, particularly by law.

Gorgon: any one of three sister monsters in Greek mythology who had snakes for hair and who could turn anyone looking at them into stone.

hierarchical: belonging to a system of persons ranked one above another.

incentives: rewards given to encourage a person to perform a task or action.

indigenous: native to and characteristic of a particular region or country.

inheritance: a person's property or money that is given to his or her friends or family when the person dies.

inhospitable: offering no shelter; barren.

liberation: the act becoming free.

nationalized: to bring under the ownership or control of a nation

petrogyphs: designs carved into rock by ancient peoples.

philanthropic: describing the quality of giving money or aid and expecting nothing in return.

portioned: divided out.

regime: a government in power.

sanctions: economic measures, often involving cutting off trade, taken by one country against another to show disapproval.

sand dunes: large, high piles of sand.

slaughtered: to kill cattle or sheep for food.

steppes: a large area of treeless grassland.

Tamazight: a language spoken by the Berber, Tuareg, and other peoples living in North Africa.

venerated: treated with great respect; honored.

vocational: relating to a trade.

More Books to Read

Libya. Cultures of the World series. Peter Malcolm (Benchmark Books)

Libya: Desert Land in Conflict. Ted Gottfried (Millbook Press)

Libya. Enchantment of the World second series. Terri Willis (Children's Book Press)

Libya in Pictures. Visual Geography Series. (Lerner Publications Company)

Libya. Major World Nations series. Renfield Sanders (Chelsea House)

Libya. Modern Middle East Nations and Their Strategic Place in the World series.
　　Daniel E. Harmon (Mason Crest Publishers)

Sahara. Vanishing Cultures series. Jan Reynolds (Bt Bound)

The Sahara and Its People. People and Places series. Simon Scoones (Thomson Learning)

Tuaregs. Endangered Cultures. Ann Carey Sabbah (Smart Apple Media)

Videos

Great TV News Stories: Muammar Qaddafi — Libya's Radical Ruler. (MPI Home Video)

Sahara - A Place of Extremes. (PBS Home Video)

Web Sites

ourworld.compuserve.com/homepages/dr_ibrahim_ighneiwa/culture.htm

www.arab.net/libya/

www.afro.com/kidstalk/discover/libya/libya.html

www.countryreports.org/libya.htm

www.libyana.org/

www.libyaweb.com/Photos/default.html

Due to the dynamic nature of the Internet, some web sites stay current longer than others. To find additional web sites, use a reliable search engine with one or more of the following keywords to help you locate information about Libya. Keywords: *Benghazi, Cyrenaica, Fezzan, Qadhafi, Septimus Sverus, Tripoli, Tripolitania, Tuareg.*

Index

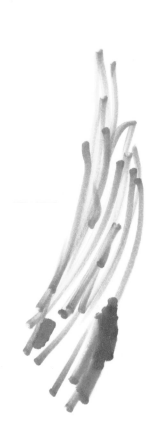